The Buddha in New York

Copyright © 2007 Michael Rosenbaum
All rights reserved.
ISBN: 1-4196-6517-0
ISBN-13: 978-1419665172

Visit www.booksurge.com to order additional copies.

The Buddha in New York

Michael Rosenbaum

2007

The Buddha in New York

CONTENTS

Introduction	xiii
Grand Central Station	1
Shoeshine	5
Just Watch Me Shuffle	7
Subway Savior	13
The Buddha at Ground Zero	19
Enter America	23
Ice	31
Fruit Sellers	35
The Church: The Essence of the Buddha	39
Ice Skating: Spray of Ice	43
Secret Dream	49
State Fair: You a Full-Time Artist?	57
Emergency Medical Team: Velcro Straps Around Her Chin	73
The Police Arrive: I'll Clear the Crowd	75
The Race Down Fifth Avenue: Sirens Wail Like Hungry Children	79
Emergency Room: Ok, Let's Go	83
The Hospital: The Waiting Room	87
The Hospital: The Room	95
The Hospital Room: Why Live?	101
The Home at the End of the Tunnel: The Mole People	107
Figure the Odds	117
Your Pockets Are There to Remind Me	121
The Little Fish Come Out Blind	123
Druggie Supermarket	127
It Gives Life or Death	129
Times Square: Crossroads of the World	135
The Situation: Checkmate	137
Wall Street	155

The Statue: A Homecoming	163
Brooklyn: Cross to the Promised Land	169
Sit Boy-Girl	189
Leaving Together	191
Set the Stage	199
Real Party Animal	209
Jewelry from Around the World	213
The Party: Full Circle	217
The Parting	223

To my very best friend, Maj-Britt

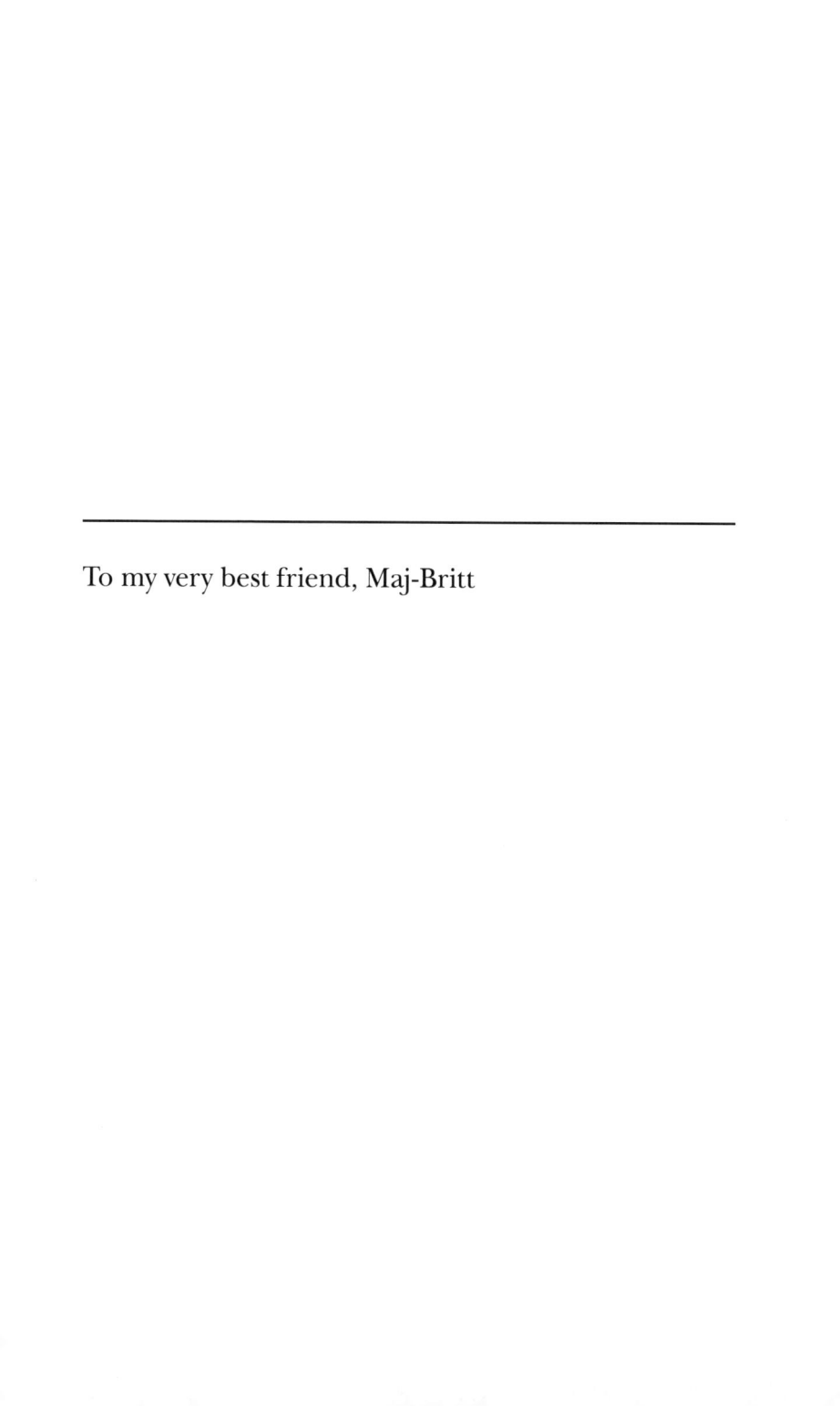

Introduction

The Buddha was engulfed. People filled the loft. Giant metal statues were planted like trees throughout the studio. He stared out the floor-to-ceiling windows at the man-made grandeur of the New York City skyline. He was far from his village and the palace of the king, which itself reached just sixty feet, not a hundred stories. He turned and gazed uptown at the blinking white lights strung in a gentle arc on the George Washington Bridge. He noticed the occasional red lights glaring as a warning to overhead planes.

A young woman motioned for all the guests to sit down and then, turning to the Buddha she said, "Your words are few but worthy, so please, we are all listening."

The Buddha, cradling a gleaming silver object, stood up to address the crowd. He nodded at several of the guests whom he had come to love as he traveled through the city. Closing his eyes for several seconds, he saw the slow-moving brown river of his village. A river not crossed by giant bridges. It was not crossed except by canoes or rafts with strong wooden paddles. With his eyes tightly shut, he recalled his voyages around New York.

The Buddha in New York   [1]

Grand Central Station

The Buddha found himself under a ceiling of painted stars in the cavernous space of Grand Central Station. He wondered, "How can this many people all walk in different directions, with no pathways or signposts, without bumping into each other, without looking at each other?"

He noticed a woman striding through the crowd in a tight black dress, her little boy out ahead of her on a leash. She walked with her head at a slight upward tilt, her jaw aimed at an invisible spot ten feet above the child's head. Just beyond them, two young men plodded along like ancient insects, hauling huge backpacks. Most people hurried through the vast space, while others seemed to linger, already at their destination.

Along one wall, three black men were seated, facing the moving human current. In front of each of them sat an empty paper coffee cup with a Greek pattern on it. Like an orchestra leader, one man would occasionally shake his cup, rattling the coins inside. Another of the men munched on a stale bagel. A few people dropped coins in the men's cups, never breaking stride. Waves of passers-by gazed at a lottery sign that read "Instant Winners!" that was situated just above the three men.

The Buddha sat down near these three, and folded his legs underneath himself as he had done for twenty-nine hundred years. Resting his hands palms-up on his knees, he closed his eyes. The three men, he mused, although sitting like fishermen, were men fishing for money. As he sat, he remembered a time back in his own country long ago when he rested on an embankment rising up from the middle of a series of underwater fields. The fields were surrounded by neatly cropped stalks of rice, and sub-divided into squares ponds where fish lived. Though the Buddha did not eat the fish, he knew they made up a substantial portion of the villagers' diet. They tended to the fish, dropping grains of rice into each brown square puddle every second day.

One time the largest fish spoke to the Buddha, "Dear Master, please send a giant wind to tear away the fine-knit wall of rice reeds so we can all swim to the great sea."

"If the walls were torn down, would you not leave, but be gulped down by crocodiles that would glide in?" the Buddha replied. "For this is your home; the villagers feed you rice. Are not miracles achieved, often more dangerous than dreams denied? So, I do not perform miracles."

On the other side of the terminal, the Buddha saw men gliding up and down a staircase without moving their legs. A woman carrying a huge bunch of flowers pushed through the moving-men down to the great floor of the terminal. The Buddha could see them all without really looking at them.

The closest of the three black men had used his sprawled leg to push one of the cups in front of the Buddha. Another of the group scooped out all the coins from the cups, pocketed some and then deposited two or three back into each cup. The Buddha reflected, "This is like the farmers in my village who, after the harvest, drop seeds back to the ground for the next season."

An indistinct voice echoed off the walls, "Train on track to Stam running late." A little girl in a one-piece jumper began to wail. The Buddha saw a silvery balloon with a mouse face and a long string-like tail rise above the child's head toward the ceiling.

Suddenly, he felt three sharp tugs on his yellow robe. He turned to see a thin young woman with yellow hair pulled back with a brown ribbon. Her long denim skirt swept the ground and her shirt read, "Visualize world peace." Her thin arms were marked with small red bulls-eyes, each with a tiny brown center.

The Buddha recalled, "A flock of wild bees stung me once as I walked in the forest. They stung me and died guarding their queen. Is there a dark forest outside this building where the honey of wild bees can be gathered?"

Then, noticing the words on the girl's t-shirt, he thought, "I can learn from this young woman, for in all my thousands of years and hours of meditation, I have never visualized world peace. For even I cannot visualize a state that can never exist."

"Dear friend," asked the Buddha, "tell me how to visualize world peace."

"OK, but first give me some money," she retorted. Overturning one of the men's coffee cups, she swept the coins in one motion into a hidden pocket in her skirt. The orchestra leader grabbed the empty cup and waved a clenched fist at the girl. In a husky voice she shot back, "Finders keepers!"

She moved out of range of the menacing fist and squatted down on the other side of the Buddha. "Listen, first you teach me how to dance like in your country. Twirl my skirt. Show my legs. Guys will shower money on me."

"My friend, the first lesson in dance is like all the lessons that follow."

"Come on, Mister Yellow Robe, I'm not stupid. The second lesson sort of adds to the first and then with the third you build up your steps. I took ballet lessons as a kid. Wasn't bad."

"My friend, if you receive a lesson, it is always, at that moment, the first lesson."

"Let's make a deal, man. Bet you don't know much about the Big Apple. We got buildings that scrape the sky. We got long secret underground tunnels. I'll lead you on a twenty-four hour non-stop day. You just sit and say whatever. We'll split up the money from tourists." She gestured toward a massive illuminated Kodak photo of a mountain range and began pretending to take a picture of the seated Buddha. "Click. Click. Come on, get up, buddy."

"My dear young friend, please do guide me. But remember that I cannot teach you anything that you do not already know."

As the Buddha stood up, a beefy man approached him. "Hey Mister, what you doing with this charming young woman?" He then muttered under his breath, "No good druggie hooker…"

"I recognize the sweet voice of Detective Fist Class Patrick Flynn. Midtown South Vice Squad," the girl said, without turning around. Give me a fucking break. I'm clean—I'm his guide." She radiated a hint of a smile. Flynn glared back, his green polyester sport jacket taut against his massive chest, revealing a bulge near his heart. The girl stepped forward, gave him a light tap on the chest as she stared at his crotch, "Make sure it's loaded."

Shoeshine

The girl pulled the Buddha out of the train station through a wide glass door. "Check it out, Forty-second Street!" Gesturing with a dramatic sweep of her arm, she said "I'm gonna show you the town, buddy. By the way, the name's Mary. Not sure what your name is, but I'm callin' you Bud." Then, like a courtesan on a king's elbow, she took him down the busy street.

From the corner, a voice called to them, "Hey Mister, want a shine? Fine shine. First shoe free." They turned to see a man with a thin body, white hair and hands dyed black from years of work. He patted his shoeshine stand. The rectangular wooden box was topped with dirty red plastic and a raised piece of copper shaped like a foot. The Buddha smelled a perfume of soap and wax coming from the box.

"Creep, get lost," Mary muttered. "Can't you tell sandals from Shinola?"

"Just wanna get an honest dollar. Ever heard of an honest dollar?"

Just then, the Buddha freed his feet from his shoes with

two quick flicks of his ankles. He bent down gracefully and handed the sandals to the shoeshine man.

"My friend, my sandals are dusty. See the frayed ends of hemp? Why should they move from their own tan to strong black?"

"My work man, my work. It's what to do."

"Well, my friend, do the second sandal first. Soon I will return with what you need or what you desire."

While the Buddha was talking, the man had coated both sandals with a clear liquid. "See 'em shine. I'm too poor for any old desire. You'll never come back. Give me what I need: money. Whatever you want. Got to eat, you know."

Turning to Mary, the Buddha said, "Please give him some of the coins you harvested from the cups."

She shook her head and the Buddha gazed at her until she reached into her dress, pulling out a single coin.

"Here you go. Enjoy yourself, Shineman."

The Buddha continued to stare at her, a slight smile on his lips.

"OK, OK," she relented. She extracted two more coins and dropped them in front of the shoeshine man who trapped them as they started to roll. "Listen Bud, if we shell out to every bum on the street, we'll starve."

The Buddha countered, "Who has ever starved from sharing? Neither the mother bird nor the baby bird. The more the baby eats, the more the mother finds."

"I hope you're right 'cause in this city, birds push each other out of the nest—that is if they even have a nest. Let's go."

Just Watch Me Shuffle

As the two walked along, they came upon a young man wearing a sport shirt with red hibiscus flowers on it. He was nervously eyeing two men standing about fifteen feet away. One of the men had a long-sleeved white t-shirt and a "Viva Puerto Rico" baseball hat, while the other wore a matching hibiscus-patterned sport shirt. The two men stood on either side of a long thin cardboard box resting on two metal trashcans.

The man in the hat by the makeshift table began to yell in an excited voice to no one, "I win man. It's easy! I win ten bucks on the black ace."

The Buddha saw the winner's face reflected in the huge glass store window across the table from him. A sign along the upper length of the window read, "SUMMER BLOW OUT SALE—50% OFF!" The sale shoes were lined up like neat rows of soldiers with uniforms of bright purple, silky silver and soft pink. Most had thick soles of cork and a steep angle for the foot. The Buddha saw Mary staring at the shoes. He then noticed that on her feet she had black basketball shoes with untied laces and jagged tears near the little toes.

The Buddha edged closer to the two men. The winner placed a ten-dollar bill on the table. The dealer dropped three cards face upon the table—two red and one black.

"Pick the black and win. Just watch me shuffle." He picked up the cards one at a time with elaborate care, his hands moving in small intersecting circles. Then he opened his left hand, allowing the cards to flutter one at a time, dropping to the cardboard.

The player clapped his hands together like a one-man cheering section. Pointing to the card on the left, he cried, "Another ten bucks! Oh baby, I'm the greatest! My eyes so quick, beat his hands all day long." He grabbed the money and placed it in the pocket of his flowered shirt.

Three men with dark suits and soft leather briefcases watched over the excited winner's shoulder. One whispered to the other, "I saw it too. We can beat this guy."

The winner waved the bills in front of the three men with a happy whistle and sauntered up the street, winking at his red-shirted twin.

Mary pushed toward the cardboard table. After a quick simple shuffle, the dealer dropped the three cards facedown. Mary nudged the Buddha, "Hey, Bud. It's the card on the left. You like to bet?"

The Buddha gently held her hand. "My friend, I do not gamble. When my eyes are open, they see the world just like you. They see traffic lights turn colors and mirrors turn letters around. When my eyes are open, they can be fooled just like yours. When I close my eyes, I see clearly what really is. Can you see the strength of the river rushing down when you scoop out water and look at it in your hands?"

Pulling the Buddha toward her, she said in a plaintive voice, "Bud, please. Please close your eyes. Tell me which card is the black ace. It's not gambling, 'cause there's no chance of losing."

Reaching down the front of her dress, she pulled out a folded bill. "Here goes," she said, dropping the bill on the table.

The dealer pushed the bill back to her with a look of disdain.

"Lady, that's one dollar. My smallest play is five. I run a class game. Need a legit minimum. Dollar betters! Better go to Harlem. Guys there deal for pennies."

One of the dark-suited men said in a commanding voice, "Give her a break. This is not exactly Caesar's Palace. No dancing girls, no rent, no taxes. Take her onesy. I'm putting a ten spot on my pick."

His voice drowned out the cars honking at a double-parked newspaper truck, its driver throwing out bales of tightly bound papers.

The dealer muttered to himself, "Girl beats paying another shill. Let's go, suckers."

He showed the two red cards and the black ace and then turned them over. With a single slow shuffle, he dropped each of them facedown in a row.

Ignoring Mary, he said in a singsong chant, "It's easy. So easy. Pick the black ace to win. You're the big better, Mister Businessman. Pick it. You know the ace is on the left. You got sharp eyes. I'll make it easier for my best customer." He reached down and turned up a red card in the middle.

The man had a hot dog soaked in catsup, mustard and onions in one hand. He used his other hand—the one holding his gold-initialed briefcase—to point to the card on the left.

The dealer turned over the man's pick. "Tough luck," he said with false sympathy as he revealed the second red card. He swooped up the man's ten-dollar bill.

The dealer turned to Mary, handing her a dollar. "Here lady, you bring me luck. I let you play for under the house minimum. Just pull out some more treasure from that terrific chest."

Mary first wiped her hand on her head and then reached down into the front of her dress. Her hand glided down toward her breasts. A fist full of bills emerged, and her dress hung straight down from her now deflated chest. With a deliberate slowness, she smoothed them out.

"Two. Three. Four. Five. Six. Seven. Eight. That's it. All the money I got in the world. Here goes," she said hopefully. She ceremoniously placed the eight dollars next to the two singles on the table.

The dealer shuffled the three cards high above the makeshift table. He raised and lowered both arms as if to signal a call to prayer, oblivious to people pushing past his game without even a momentary glance up at his exaggerated movements.

The Buddha watched him and remembered, "Once along the riverbank in a village a day's walk from the main road, I had seen a wandering sage perform a similar ritual. The sage had three large clamshells and a small shiny black stone. He entertained the children by moving the shells back and forth very quickly so that the stone was batted from one shell to another. He would turn over the shells after the children guessed which one covered the stone. Again and again he shuffled the stone from shell to shell.

"I heard the sage say, 'Dear children, eyes that look outward see only a glimmer of reality and are many times fooled. Look inward. See the spirit.'

"A boy of ten smiled and closed his eyes. 'When I am a man I will follow you,' he said.

"Three other children standing nearby also closed their eyes. They sang in unison, 'Dear sage, can we come too? Can we come too?'

"The elder of the village approached the sage and angrily threw some coins at him. 'Don't bother us again, old man. Let the children work in the fields and not hear your foolishness. If you come again we will not throw coins but sticks. Be gone.'

"As the sage scurried away, clutching the coins and his shells, he approached me and asked, 'Master, my life is to teach children. What shall I do?'

"I replied, 'There are villages without limit and children in them all. You have much work to do. Remember these children are like water flowing through our lives. They learn from the encounter. Then they are gone. We never meet them again. So continue your walk.'"

The Buddha stood at the table with his eyes wide open. He stared at the glass wall beneath the huge shoe sign. He gave Mary's hand a squeeze and nodded his head upward. Mary followed his gaze.

"I cannot help you," he said, "as you must see for yourself."

She scoured the large storefront, and then let her focus drop to the glass wall angled down on the dealer. She suppressed a huge smile as she saw the back of the dealer and the faces of the three hidden cards reflected in the plate glass window.

The dealer asked impatiently, "Which card, lady?"

Mary's hand hovered over the three cards as if she were unsure. Then she reached down and turned over the black ace.

"I won!" she cried.

The dealer was shocked. He implored her, "Play again. Double or nothing. You got the touch."

"No thanks, we're leaving." She pulled the Buddha's hand. "Come on. Let's take the subway to see the lady who greets all you foreigners—the Statue of Liberty."

Subway Savior

As the Buddha entered the subway, a stream of moist, pungent air greeted him. "It is like under a green jungle canopy, but I see no plants."

"Yeah, it's a jungle where nothing lives," replied Mary. "Lotsa strange creatures down here. Look at that guy."

The Buddha saw a man approaching them with a simple hand-lettered sign that read, "Eternal Life."

He walked right up to them and then, leaning toward Mary, he said, "Do you want eternal life? Wanna join all your friends in heaven? You can have your soul live forever. Yes, forever and forever! Join with God."

He thrust his head forward toward her like an old-fashioned marine drill sergeant until their faces nearly touched. "Are you really listening? Say, are you a God-fearing Christian or some kind of hippie? Are you with that brown guy in the yellow robe?"

The man's questions roared over the mechanical subway announcements emanating from two huge overhead speakers suspended from wires at each end of the platform. The recordings in each speaker were just out of synch, so it sounded like a choir. "The A train is not running at the present time on the express track, so all passengers must use the local track. We regret any inconvenience. The A train is not running. Use track…Regret…Train is not running…Regret."

Mary took two steps back from the man so his ranting was bearable and to reduce his breath of chili hot dogs.

"Eternal life, like the holy saints," he continued over the din of the speakers.

"Yeah, yeah, yeah. I'm a born Christian, a living hippie. Giving old Yellow Robe a magic tour of our city. So, you sell eternal life?"

Just then, a fat black cop walked by whistling Dixie. The cop twirled his baton, ignoring this trio that by his subway standards looked normal and harmless.

"Yes, I promise eternal life. I don't sell what God gives freely. Your body will never rot and your soul will remain pure. What does he promise you, Miss Tour Guide?"

Mary shook her head from side to side, "A major rehab to make my soul pure. My old body looks like it's already got the rot going. See the wrinkles on my forehead? Last year, pure baby skin. Today, permanent-press creases. Tomorrow I'll look like a living checkerboard."

She half-turned to face the Buddha and cupped his ear to overcome the screeching of the trains. "If I follow this guy, my soul is saved, I hop up to heaven, my body won't rot and I'll live forever. What you got to offer if I follow you? What's the word? What can you tell me?"

The Buddha gave a slow, formal nod first to the man and then to Mary. "Sir, and my dear young friend, you both speak from the heart. You have answers to the eternal questions and you have questions seeking eternal answers."

There were a series of metallic shrieks as a train stopped. The double doors in front of the Buddha opened only partially. People popped out one at a time like human champagne corks propelled forward by the crowd pushing from behind.

"Get out of de way, religious faggots," yelled a muscular teenager in a black Harley Davidson t-shirt.

The conductor stuck his head out the window. He wore a blue wool cap pulled down to his ears, Walkman headphones and yellow-tinted ski glasses. He snapped his fingers to a secret tune only he heard and stole furtive glances at the automatic doors as they opened and closed on the back of the last passenger crowding into the train.

The Buddha continued, "I do not know if the soul is eternal or if the soul is not eternal. I do not know if the bodies of the saints rot or if they do not rot. I do not know whether or not you will meet your friends in heaven, or if there is or is not a heaven. For all these questions and many more I have no answers. The questions are not important to me and I do not try to give answers to them. These are simply words strung together without regard to life. Those who follow me follow me in life."

Three teenage girls standing nearby belted out a rap song accompanied by enthusiastic handclapping.

"Speak up, I can't hear you over that heavenly choir," Mary barked.

"I do know that we were all born, we all live and we all will die. Those who travel with me will learn about life. That is all there is. That is all I know."

The human tide had turned. People were now pushing to get into the subway car. Mary grabbed the Buddha's hand and pulled him toward the half-open doors. She shouted back to the man on the platform, "Pray for my eternal soul, Mister. You could be right on." She turned back to the Buddha as the doors closed and said, "You don't offer me a sure thing like old Save-a-Sign back there, but let's follow and lead each other. What will a pair like us find in New York? Who knows? Who even cares? We're off."

But the train didn't move. The conductor saw a wide yellow swatch of cloth fluttering outside the closed car door. "Damn," he thought. "Some lady'll start yelling that I closed the door on her butt and ruined her most expensive dress. My supervisor'll give me bad marks."

He opened the doors to his car and moved quickly down the platform swinging a ring of keys in one hand and snapping his fingers with the other.

"Get going! Move your ass. Get this thing outta here!" With a quick turn of a key, the doors holding the Buddha's robe popped open. "Damn, a man with a robe," he thought. "Listen, Mister, you delay this train, you piss 'em all off. You get your insides squeezed if your robe catches on a light or something in the tunnel. You got no sense to know if your clothes is inside or out. Where you from? You never see a subway? Go up and get some air." He stuck a token into the Buddha's hand.

The Buddha nodded, "I thank you for the coin and your concern for air. For air in tunnels is like water that knows no tide. You have put me on the right path. I shall travel through your city in the air. The Buddha extended his arm with his hand open cradling the coin. "Please take your generous gift back. Give it instead to a friend who needs to travel in the tunnel. If I keep it and do not use it, that is useless and selfish excess. For me, this coin would be a souvenir, but I will remember your kindness even without its presence."

Mary shook her head in disgust, grabbed the token and pulled the Buddha out of the car. "Listen, man, we have a few bucks in our jeans, but let's not play Santa. You know who Santa is? That's his turf. Another whole religion. Oh forget it. Let's walk. Air he wants to see. Hold your breath till we're out of this tunnel."

The conductor shrugged his shoulders to the packed passengers in the car, "Our motto at the New York City Transit Authority is, 'The customer is always right.' He wants clean air to breath? Let him speak to the environmental protection boys."

"Shut up and get the train moving. I'm late 'cause of that weirdo!" shouted an invisible voice from the Greek choir inside the car.

"Get a soapbox!"

"Save your deep insights for your break!"
"Get your ass in gear!"

The conductor turned the key closing the door. He walked with small careful steps toward the front of the train.

The recorded voice over the PA system was stuck like an old scratchy record, "We regret at the present time...We regret at the present time...We regret..."

The conductor reflected, "I give all my records to my church. They give them to really poor folk. Next year, I'll give 'em all my tapes. In five years, I'll give every last CD. Big-time charity. I'll be generous like my friend in the yellow robe."

With a toot of the whistle and a starting screech, the subway train hurtled into darkness. "Yeah," he thought, "maybe seeing live bodies bustling around is better for the soul than staring down a dark tunnel. No more secret symphony from my portable CD player, my body floating in a lake of sound and blackness."

The conductor shook his head. "That guy in the robe is right on. I can drive a huge bus up in the air on those beautiful city streets. The taxis sneaking into lanes marked for buses only, pedestrians viewing "Don't Walk" signs as a challenge and not a municipal command, honkers who must believe in magic. Their random symphony causes cars to move like chariots."

At the stop at the end of Manhattan, he saw the Buddha in his yellow robes, walking up the platform. "Too bad that druggie girl with her scratched up arm grabbed the token. I'd have put it on a leather thong and worn it like a souvenir from the guy who made me ascend into the air. Wait till I tell the old lady a funny guy in a yellow robe changed me from a mole in a tunnel to a man in the air."

The Buddha at Ground Zero

Mary said to the Buddha, "There's a new tourist attraction. The opposite of the Statue of Liberty." She stopped walking and turned to face the Buddha.

"Yes, the Statue of Liberty is the symbol of hope. You are speaking of the opposite—Ground Zero. I have the obligation to see it as well." The slight breeze had ended. The Buddha's robe hung down around him, like a shroud.

As they approached Ground Zero, they saw tables filled with photos: Lower Manhattan prior to 9/11 with the dominant thrust of the Twin Towers; two dark beams of intense blue light emerging from the earth, a skyline filled with dense, whitish smoke.

"Hurry up," Mary said, "I can't stand to look at the photos."

"Yes, instead we will stare at the reality," the Buddha replied.

"There is a visitors' walkway. You get a good view—a horrible view." She pulled him by the hand toward the walkway. There was a line of several hundred people on the sidewalk, moving very slowly and quietly ahead. No pushing.

Even children waiting with their parents were subdued with mask-like faces—not radiant, not expressive.

Mary remembered when she was seven years old, her father had taken her to the state capital for the funeral of the Governor who had been a distant cousin. Broad marble steps led up to a rotunda. Solemn-faced policemen were lined up on each side of the stairway. A red velvet rope mounted on plain black wooden posts hemmed in the crowd mounting the stairs. With no sound and no pushing, the line progressed upward. Her father held her hand as she entered the rotunda toward the coffin surrounded by flowers. At the coffin, some nodded their heads, some crossed themselves and some leaned forward crying. Mary shut her eyes and did not open them until she heard her father say, "Be careful. We're going down the steps now."

They peered down from the viewing platform to the acres of cavernous space. "Have you ever seen anything so terrible?" Mary asked, pushing her face into the Buddha's robe so he could not see her start to cry.

"Yes. Quite near my country there was a madman who turned his land into a giant killing field. He killed all. Old, young, men, women. Even small children."

"Why did he do that? What was his purpose?" She had wiped her face dry on his robe and poured her eyes into his.

"I do not know."

Mary pointed her arm toward the center of Ground Zero. "Who can explain the hate? Who knows why someone took the subway to work on time and died and someone missed a train and lived?"

"I do not know."

"But you look like someone who should know," she protested. "I heard priests and rabbis and ministers on TV. They all had something to say. Some believed in God more. Some said their faith was shattered. Say something to me, please."

"Yes, my dear friend." The Buddha reached into his robe and pulled out a plain white envelope. "I have carried this letter from my country. I have two copies. Let us paste one up on that board covered with messages. After the rain washes all of them down, we can come back and put up another." He pulled out one copy and handed it to her.

The message board was an unkempt mosaic of paper held together by Scotch tape, staples and thumbtacks. Photos made from colored Xeroxes dripped rainbow shades of ink down to words in bold black print: "MISSING," or "FATHER" or simply "REMEMBER." Names, phone numbers, emails or addresses were sprinkled on each sheet.

She unfolded the letter and found a few thumbtacks that no longer held a message. "Here. It's up. Please read it to me. Your handwriting is OK, but I'd like to hear your voice."

"Certainly, my dear friend." The Buddha stepped forward and began to speak in a quiet voice.

Who lives in darkness flashing hate?
Who dances in sunshine smiling?

Why do paths cross in ways we cannot trace?
Why do lives mingle?

Bodies embrace in love
Bodies collide in terror

How many shall be crossed out?
How many shall be created?

Who shall be rested in his home?
Who shall be wrested from his home?

The path winds up to the mountain inn
So we can see the pattern down below

[22]   Michael Rosenbaum

From our perch we descend
To begin another day
To plant another seed

Enter America

As they got off the ferry, Mary pointed to the huge building that dominated Ellis Island. "Look. I've seen the inside once. It's interesting, but once is enough. Go by yourself. I'll sit out here, bum a smoke and watch the birds and the boats. Take your time."

The Buddha started up the path to the building.

A large man stood before him.

"Can I help you, Mister?"

The Buddha smiled, for he knew the man did not want to help him.

"May I enter to join a tour of your wonderful building?" he asked softly. He waited for the answer, placing his hands within the folds of his robe.

"Visitors are welcome, but if you bring drugs, you get locked up big-time. Know what I mean? I'm a detective. Detective Leary. How much money you got on you?"

"I do not travel with money," replied the Buddha

"Sweet Jesus! Even those black coat Orthodox carry money six days a week. So what do you do? Beg or deal? Not in my town, buddy boy. Can I search your robe? See if you got little packets?"

"Dear friend, I do not beg, but in my country, the villagers give me food and let me share their room. I do not deal. I do not play cards. Please touch my robes as you please. If I laugh, I am not rude, but ticklish."

Leary pulled back his hands quickly as if they had been spared from poking around in a primordial ooze. "OK, OK. Keep clean. Last month, six phony monks in orange robes were dealing. Now they play solitaire in solitaire." Leary's belly swung up and down as he laughed at his own joke. He straightened up his tight-fitting jacket and smiled. "Go right in, but I'm watching you. Don't worry about getting lost, 'cause I'll be right there to get you on the right track."

The Grand Hall of Ellis Island enveloped the Buddha. In the middle of the massive space, he saw a long row of suitcases piled high, forming a wall. Beyond that were huge black and white photos of early immigrants. He turned to Leary who was standing three steps away with a bored look on his face.

"In my voyages around the earth, I have never seen a room to welcome strangers. In my country, the villagers invite the traveler to share a simple meal, but the king guards his border with searches and suspicion."

"No kings in the U.S. of A.," said Leary.

The Buddha walked toward a photo full of women whose faces peered out from flowery bonnets.

"I have read that all came to seek a better life. Why did your father come?"

Flustered by the question, Leary rubbed his massive hands together for a few moments in silence. "My great-great grandfather came from Ireland. Damn British beat us! Worked us like slaves." Leary stopped. He bellowed at a young woman across the room with an unlit cigarette hanging from her mouth, "Hey you! Yeah, you. Can't you read? No smoking, sweetheart." He pulled out his wallet, flashing a gold badge at the startled youth. "I oughta bust her. No respect. Anyway

Mister, the potato famine—when it came, they left us to starve in the streets. Now I'm the law, not some politician sitting in some committee room voting on this word and that."

He paused and smiled, "I'm the law on the street. I make the law when I walk the street. It's a better life. Real better. That's what I think. That's what I know."

The Buddha replied, "We are what we think. Everything comes from our thoughts. If we say 'He starved me and beat me' and live with such thoughts, we live in hate. If we say, 'He starved me and beat me' and abandon such thoughts, we live in love."

Leary shuffled his feet. The Buddha continued, "What is the better life, dear friend? What is the better life?" The Buddha gave Leary a wisp of a smile and walked toward a wide staircase leading up to the Registry Room.

There he stood silently and listened to a tour guide. She was speaking to a group of schoolgirls all sporting tiny nametags and dressed in dark green skirts and white blouses. The guide stared at the nametags for an instant. "Now Monica, have you ever visited a doctor?" The girl nodded her head up and down. "All the new immigrants walked up these stairs. Doctors stared down at them. If they had trouble walking…" the guide continued.

"Cripples!" giggled Monica.

"If they got out of breath…"

"Bad hearts!"

A classmate poked Monica in the ribs, "Shut up! You some kind of doctor?"

"You shut up!" said Monica. "I can be a doctor and you'll just sell fruit all day from a cart." Monica laughed and grabbed her friend's hand.

The guide ignored these comments and pressed ahead, "If they had funny expressions on their faces…"

"Fruitcakes," whispered Monica. The schoolgirls began to laugh.

Even the stern-faced tour guide was forced to smile. "You are a very attentive group. Well, the doctors would pull them aside and chalk a big high 'X' on their right shoulder for suspected mental defects. A chalk X low on the right shoulder meant the person had some disease or was crippled. An X within a circle meant a specific disease had been detected. Everyone marked with an X would be given a careful physical or mental exam."

"Does it take a long time when you visit a doctor?" the guide asked Monica.

"It takes too long. All that poking around. Yuck!"

"Well, at Ellis Island, each doctor spent six seconds examining each person. Six seconds which could decide whether they'd enter America or be shipped back to their home country."

"That's more stupid than the ER. Why so fast? Me and my mom wait maybe two hours in the ER. I bring my homework," said the brown-skinned girl with shiny black hair holding Monica's hand. In her free hand she held a small paper bag, bulging with green apples.

The guide with a quick glimpse at the nametag replied, "Well, Yael, too many people and too few doctors. In 1850, before Ellis Island was open, nearly two thousand ships delivered 212,796 newcomers to a three-mile stretch of docks along the Hudson and East River. Think of it. Today, the Bronx has over two million. In 1850, there were less than two hundred fifty thousand. Imagine everyone in the Bronx: men, women and children, arriving from all over the world, with no money, often no family here and not speaking English."

The Buddha reflected on the medical exams, "In my village, there were no doctors. A sick person would sit alone with a grandmother in a special hut. He would sit for an hour or sit for a day. The grandmother listened, rarely speaking. When sick people left, they all felt better. Some got better. Some got worse, but in six seconds, one cannot listen. Not to the person. Not even to the heart."

At the top of the stairs, the Buddha looked through the huge arched windows of the Registry Room. He saw the Statue of Liberty clad in green, looking directly at Ellis Island. Through another window, he saw the wall of buildings forming lower Manhattan reflecting the sunlight and waves from their glass facades. He sat down on a faded wooden bench that the immigrants had rested on while awaiting the next step on their entrance maze. He observed men in business suits whispering to other men in white robes and flowing Arab headdresses, muted sounds leaking out of their earphones.

"So we meet again, Mister. Taking a breather?" asked Leary.

As the Buddha began to answer, the jarring sound of a boom box drowned out his reply. Leary shot an angry look at a muscular young man dressed in black jeans and a black leather jacket. He stood holding the boom box in one hand and snapping his fingers with the other.

Leary flashed his badge and yelled over the music, "Turn that off, or I'll bust you for disturbing the peace." He then muttered to himself, "Punks. No fucking respect."

With a smirk, the young man turned the volume down to a whisper.

Leary turned to face the Buddha. "Listen, tell me. Why'd you come here? I mean, to the States?"

"Dear Officer, just like that young man you ordered silenced, I am looking for America."

The young man laughed as he retreated a few steps, "That's it, baby. Tell the man. You dig this music. Play the whole tape for you on the ferry back." He grinned at the Buddha and pumped up his free hand like a boxer delivering a knockout punch.

Leary retorted, "Get lost creep." Then he said to the Buddha, "See you around, Mister."

Finding himself alone, the Buddha placed his hands palms-up on his lap and closed his eyes. The silence was broken by an irregular clatter like carts dragging sheets of metal in a circle. He opened his eyes to see a helicopter motionless about fifty feet from the top of the building. The helicopter landed, and picked up the group of men clad in suits and white robes.

With an upward lurch, it started to move toward lower Manhattan, leaving the Great Hall quiet except for the shouts of the schoolchildren whose tour group was fast approaching him.

"Those with chalk Xs sat here for a mental or physical exam," the guide noted, pointing to the bench where the Buddha was seated.

"Why is that guy sitting there? What's wrong with him?" asked Monica.

The guide gave the Buddha a weak apologetic smile.

"Nearly ninety-eight percent of the new arrivals passed the tests and entered the United States. Everyone was scared. These were the biggest tests of their lives."

"Yeah, dumb multiple choice tests scare me, but I pass," Monica moaned.

"Here's what a doctor said of a young girl who was sent back because she had a slight limp, 'She died of heartbreak. She strained to look out a dusty window to see what she knew she could never possess.'"

For once the children remained silent. The Buddha closed his eyes.

He remembered looking through a narrow window at a large palace, and thought to himself, "I gazed up at the palace of my father with its turrets cloaked in gold. It is not iron that imprisoned me, nor rope, nor wood, but the pleasure I took in gold and jewels. I gave up desire to shake off my chains. Heartbreak, my teacher told me, takes two shapes. Not getting what you want or getting it."

After sitting quietly for a few minutes, the Buddha arose and continued his tour. He wandered into a room labeled, "Treasures from Home." The schoolchildren were running from case to case, staring at the exhibits ranging from elaborate silver jewelry to leather-bound books. He lifted the headphones to his ear and heard an immigrant voice proclaim, "To escape the Czar, I walked for twenty-three days. I carried with me candles and my Bible. For I knew in America, everything was possible."

The Buddha saw a flock of seagulls making a lazy pattern over the water.

"Bet they want to eat," said Yael turning to the Buddha. "Birds always want to eat. Wish I could fly. Beats walking. I'd never carry books for weeks. No way. What you thinking, Mister?"

The Buddha smiled, for he had walked through many seasons. "I carried no holy book, but I stopped in many villages. They gathered around me to hear holy words."

"What holy words? My preacher is full of holy words," she replied.

"I said however many holy words you read. However many you speak. What good will they do if you do not act upon them? Many were disappointed, for they wanted to memorize and answer and not live. Not live in this world."

"You're not like my minister. You're something else," Yael giggled. "Bye, Mister. Want an apple? My dad gives me fruit. I hate it." She handed an apple to the Buddha who accepted it with a bow.

Ice

As they walked up the subway stairs, the Buddha blinked in the hazy light of the street. The air was warm but not moist like in the tunnel.

Mary turned to him, "You ever ice skated? You ever see ice?"

"I have seen in a picture book girls ice skating. They looked like birds ready to take flight, but I have never seen ice. Once in my country, an old man told me he had seen ice in a box of thick wood. It wrapped in layers of fine silk that a sage carried from village to village. The ice, he told me, was colder than any stone at night. He had touched it. He had squeezed it so hard that it dripped water like tears. When the sage reached my village, he beat on a large brass gong. Soon the entire village surrounded this box and the sage proclaimed, 'I have ice which grows at the top of our tallest mountains. In the valleys, it is delicate, so I protect it from its enemy, the sun. Now who would like to see it? To touch it? Do not be afraid. It is not poisonous. You—,' he pointed to a young boy.

"Opening the lid, he said to the child, 'Put your hand in

and look inside. Be quick.' But the boy ran away in tears and hid behind his mother.

"All in the village looked at me. 'Oh, Master, look and tell us,' the mother cried, and the crowd chanted for me to do so.

"I walked up to the sage and bowed. 'Dear Sage,' I said, 'I shall search for the boy who is too fearful to look. After I do, all in the village will look on your wondrous ice.' The villagers began to form a line with the smallest children at the front and the old men at the rear. The children were silent, for they knew I would not permit harm to befall them.

"I looked inside and lowered my hands into the box. 'Dear sage, I see what I already know, and that is water. Your ice has vanished like the wind. I am certain that it was there. When we do not act in a timely manner, then the time is gone. The action becomes an empty gesture. We have all learned that fear can cheat us. We all thank you for this lesson. Come children, touch the water with your own hands. Learn that ice and water are divided by time and the power of our sun.'"

"Great story," Mary smiled. "Yeah, so it's hot in your old village. I'll show you ice. We'll go up Fifth Avenue. They grow ice in summer. For real. Every hour a guy comes out riding a tiny truck and sort of cuts away the new tender crop just like cutting grass on a golf course. Well, you don't know from golf."

A short man hidden behind half a dozen boxed pizzas bumped into the Buddha, but grabbed his aromatic cargo before it slipped away, "Sorry, Mister. Hard to see."

Mary pulled the Buddha behind her on the crowded sidewalk, forcing pedestrians to either veer to the side or be impaled on her elbow that extended like the prow of a Viking ship. At a red light, she slowed down and pulled the Buddha alongside her. "Now, I know ice. See, in Nebraska, where I grew up, there aren't a bunch of lakes or ponds, but it is flat. So two days before Thanksgiving, they'd turn the fire hose on the high school basketball court. Spray water on it all afternoon. Then before pigging out on turkey, we'd all get dressed sort of fancy but warm and go skating. I'd wear two wool homemade sweaters under my red parka, a little striped ballerina skirt and two pairs of real tight leggings."

Mary noticed the somber look on the Buddha's face, "Hey, I know that you're probably not a meat-eating type, but here we eat cows and pigs and turkeys. Did you ever visit a country where if you screw a pig you go to jail, but if you raise it like a pet, kill it and eat it, that's OK? The American Way! Strange customs, these locals."

The Buddha smiled as they continued on their way.

Fruit Sellers

"Come on, Bud, we're almost there," Mary cried.

Glittering office buildings reflected sunlight like broken beacons from the heights to the street below. Despite this urban landscape, the Buddha was reminded of the market square in a village in his country. There were wooden carts on the crowded sidewalk overflowing with outrageously bright green silk blouses with gold and silver trim and neatly stacked CDs showing black faces huffing on trumpets or with lips wide open, deep in sound.

The Buddha saw rugs laden with silver jewelry and signs stating, "Handmade by artists. None over $10." There were t-shirts, each featuring a bitten apple and a different message. "I took a bite out of the Big Apple and lived, baby!" read one. Another said, "The Big Apple—Yes, we got no bananas."

Next he came upon a rug piled high with baskets of fruit. Sitting cross-legged next to the stacks of fruit by a wooden cart was a man, light brown, like the Buddha.

"Have I not seen this man in my country?" the Buddha reflected. He smiled as he approached the sky blue cart, with its two big wooden wheels painted a deep purple. The cart was full of baskets, each overflowing with a pyramid of mangos, bananas, or apples.

The Buddha recalled that in his village at the end of the market day, the sellers would give away fruits and vegetables on the verge of rotting to small children who wolfed them down on the spot. For if the children took them home, their mothers would yell at them for stealing. In the market square in the village by the wide river, there were also rough cloth shirts for sale bleached white for the women, purple for the men, and left a natural tan for the children. Though the villagers used coins on special occasions, with the sellers they traded—offering small pink shells strung into necklaces, or intricately carved walking sticks with dragons curving up to the top of dark polished wood. There were no signs stating, "Handmade by artists," but the Buddha mused that in each village only two or three people could read or write, and that everything was handmade anyway.

Mary shook the Buddha's shoulder gently, "These guys sell junk. T-shirts guaranteed to shrink to baby size. Fruit turns rotten in your mouth. If the jewelry is silver made by artists, I'm Madonna. The stuff is stamped in Brooklyn and waved over a can of silver paint."

The Buddha nodded and said something to the fruit seller that Mary could not understand. The seller made a bow and spread his arms palms-up over the piled fruit, offering the Buddha a gift.

Mary tugged his shoulder strongly, "Hey, man, speak English. You're in America. This looks like a scene from a spiritually uplifting grade school film, "Meet Friends from Around the World."

The Buddha took a banana and a mango, offering them to Mary. "OK, OK," she said. "Just the banana. At least I can peel the sucker. That mango's good for one stringy bite and a huge pit."

The fruit seller smiled and spoke in a deliberate manner.

His speech was musical with sharp, uplifting cadences but was unintelligible to Mary.

"So tell me, what was he singsonging about?"

The Buddha replied, "There were twelve spokes on his wheel. Each a different month. My dear friend, do you see how they all run toward the center?"

"Sure. That's how a wheel is."

"Yes, they all carry themselves to the hub. But there is nothing at the center that makes the wheel work. If you make a vase, you have to make it hollow. The emptiness within makes it useful. In a temple, house or hut, it is the empty spaces—doors, windows—which make it usable. All things use how they are made to do what they do. But without their nothingness, each of them would be nothing."

The fruit seller bowed his head to the Buddha, "I speak to you, my Master, in English. Hear me reply. You are a mighty river flowing. I a tiny puddle stuck here on a crowded sidewalk. This city, I know its paths. You guide all here and everywhere. If you lose your own way in the stone canyons, come back again for hand of small guide."

"Dear friend who gives me food and will share his wisdom, please remember that a puddle is more of a miracle than a river that thrashes about and knows not its path. A puddle always comes to rest in the earth in a hollow that exactly matches its shape."

As the Buddha walked on, he realized why the fruit seller's face was familiar. His daughter had given the Buddha an apple on Ellis Island.

The Church: The Essence of the Buddha

"Let's move right along. This guide has planned stops and sights to see. Hey, see that statue? There's one gorgeous hunk." Mary sauntered over to a huge, glittering gold statue of Atlas supporting the world. His polished knee was bent under the enormous burden resting on his shoulders.

She placed her thin arm on his knee, "You need a camera like a real tourist. Ever see a statue so big?"

A man with a cap, matching blue shirt and a tiny badge approached Mary, pounding his wooden baton against his hand, "Don't rub that knee. It don't bring luck. The knee's rubbed down to black metal so you know it's not solid gold. People keep rubbing, hoping for a miracle. Wanna hit the lotto. Not been a miracle in New York since the Mets won the World Series."

The Buddha nodded, "Outside a great temple there is a seated statue as tall as the top of Atlas' earth. Our statue is made of teak so the rains do not eat it away. In my country, the small children can climb up the statue and place a hand on the lips. Their feet create tiny trails up his chest. Why do they touch his lips? It is the cycle. His lips are worn down so he cannot speak. His body weakens as the trails grow larger. His hands resting on his knees lose their fingers. Every generation helps the statue be adored and destroyed. Every generation builds a new statue identical to the old one whose wooden remains are burned amidst the singing and prayer of crowds milling around the temple. There is no permanence. Even the gods give way to the feet of children."

An open double-decker bus rumbled by. The Buddha saw children pointing down at them and waving tiny colored flags. As the bus stopped, a man on the sidewalk yelled, "Sit down! It's dangerous to stand." He then gave a wave and snapped a picture. The bus chugged down the avenue.

"Well, here our God lasts forever," said Mary, "His body is eternal. Even ordinary bodies are placed in watertight steel boxes so they'll stay safe and sound. Safe from what? Don't ask me. Ask the next corner preacher we meet and we will meet more. I'm not sure what you believe in but you tell stories like saints do, not like preachers who have the final word and spell it out for you. You wanna see a really huge church? Right there. Come on, it won't bite you." She grabbed the Buddha's hand like an overprotective mother and tugged him toward Saint Patrick's Cathedral.

Dramatically rising spires threw off a soft reflective light and cast cooling shadows on the broad steps before the huge entrance doors. A giant circle of stained glass cluttered with blues and pinks graced the front.

The Buddha thought, "This church would tower over all the temples in my country." He closed his eyes and saw the biggest temple in the city of the king. The temple made of rose-colored sandstone was a simple rectangle about forty feet high with a flat courtyard in front. The villagers would stand around and gossip before the service and afterwards huddle in small groups to discuss what the sage had meant. Yet, the temple was the highest building in the city. Clearly twice as high as the palace of the king. Pilgrims or merchants saw the temple as a beacon directing them to the center of the city.

They entered the cathedral and heard chanting coming from a small room behind the gold-adorned altar. The Buddha stooped to enter the stone doorway. A priest with his rounded collar half-open was moving his arms upward to implore the four boys facing him to lift their voices to heaven. The youngsters' chant slurred the Latin syllables together in a pleasant, squeaky hum. The priest saw the Buddha and asked the boys to wait while he greeted their guest.

The Buddha made a slight bow and said, "In my country, the old men will gather and chant for hours as the boys run in and out of the temple. Our boys never stood still to be taught, but they learned the chants over the years."

The choirboys stared silently at the Buddha. One nudged another, whispering, "Don't laugh at his funny costume."

The Buddha smiled at the boys and continued, "Let young men play and old men sing. The music is sweeter and the temple is fuller. But our village is small and we do not work to change life. In your great city, the young do not play but dart about and the old move quickly without looking where they have been."

The priest picked up half a dozen manila folders then turned to the boys, "OK, guys, grab a hot dog, take a walk in the park, shoot hoops." Surprised by their liberation, each yelled his thanks to the Buddha and left.

The Buddha was staring at a small wooden statue of the Virgin Mary. The deep blues of her clothes set off a pale, slightly smiling face. The statue seemed a prisoner inside a dark box with a thick glass front. The priest looked at the Buddha studying the statue and his own reflection. The priest said, "It's terrible to lock up a statue of the Holy Mother, but we had a statue about the same size stolen in broad daylight. Who'd be so low? Who knows? Did a tourist pop it into a camera bag? Or did some poor homeless soul shove it under his coat? If God's house is not sacred, what does this city hold holy?"

The Buddha replied, "In a temple high up in the mountains, a sage entered on a cold winter day. He came before three small wooden Buddhas. He grabbed one, placed it on the floor and burned it.

"As the sage was warming his hands over the ashes, the temple guardian ran up to him and asked, 'What are you doing?'

"The sage replied, 'I was looking for the essence of the Buddha, but I found nothing. Should I burn the other two and continue my search?'"

The priest gave the Buddha a troubled look as he moved his files from hand to hand like giant cards.

The Buddha continued, "My dear brother, nothing is permanent that we see. Do not despair. A wooden Buddha won't pass through fire. A clay Buddha won't pass through water. An iron Buddha won't pass through a furnace. For the boys you teach, can you be the fire, the water, the furnace through which all things must pass and change? You can change with them but you cannot change for them."

"It would be nice to chat some more now," said the priest, "but see these papers?" He fanned them out. "I have to meet with the administrator to discuss all this. The devil is really in the details. Never mind. You know teaching singing is tough. Thank God I've not got the assignment to teach prayer. But please do come back."

The Buddha replied, "When you teach singing, you hear the changes. When you teach prayer, you hear nothing. That is why it is impossible to teach."

Ice Skating: Spray of Ice

Mary pulled the Buddha across the street, "Man, you move slow. We got things to see and miles to go. Let's see the kids skate. I'll buy coffee, I mean, nice hot herbal tea. See, there's the ice rink sort of down in the ground, below all the flags blowing. This is big-time class. I want a table right next to the ice. Come on."

They joined the line of little girls in short skirts and leggings. They all had skates peering out of bright canvas knapsacks. A mother waited with an impatient charge in one hand and her purse in the other.

Mary whispered to the Buddha, "Little girls in New York whine all the time: 'Get me a new dress, Mom. Buy me pizza.' I never asked my mom for anything. She wouldn't have listened anyway. Just tell me I was so lucky to have two parents who loved me. Say, are you like that priest? Miracles, walk on the water, rise from the dead and walk up to heaven?"

"Oh no, my dear friend. My miracles would be very modest. Not miracles like walking on water or walking up in the air. I mean the miracle of walking on earth. Have you not felt the grass spring up and down under your feet as you walk? In my home, I was asked by the villagers how many hours a day it was necessary to pray to have their prayers answered. I told them that it does not matter if you pray all day or not at all, for prayer is never answered. For, is there something that answers prayer? Instead, I told them, they should listen with all their strength to the wind bending the reeds when they walk and the water bubbling down the stream when they bathe and the cry of the infant seeking milk. If we hear clearly these sounds from the earth, we may enjoy the silences from beyond."

When they reached the head of the line, Mary gripped the Buddha's hand as if he were her child. A man who had been leading customers to the tiny tables around the rink approached them. He wore a tight-fitting silvery-gray jacket with brass buttons and golden braids on each shoulder. His black hair was combed straight back, slicked down and parted in the middle. He towered over Mary and the Buddha and looked down at them with disdain.

"How may I help you?" he asked with a small, forced smile.

He gazed squarely at the Buddha, ignoring Mary. He thought, "With his robes, he could be some big shot from the UN or an embassy. Christ, lucky he doesn't look like one of hose young Hare Krishna beggars with their cheap tambourines and gaudy miracle books. So many nice quiet, forgettable bars in midtown, why bring a tramp to my classy place? If I were a real pal, I'd tell him the names of that no questions asked hotel on Eighth Avenue with rates by the hour. Quick and cheap. Looks like a cheapie. Those marks on her arm didn't come from giant mosquitoes."

"Tea for two. We want that empty table right there, right next to the skaters," Mary said.

The man continued to ignore Mary and spoke directly to the Buddha, "Sir, wouldn't you prefer a quiet table in the back? You wouldn't want some young enthusiast to spray ice on your beautiful robe." He muttered to himself, "I'm doing this guy a favor. His boss could walk by and spot that chick, then goodbye Mister Shiny Robe. Back to the old country on the one way express."

"My young friend would like to be as close as possible to the skaters. If she is sprayed with ice, she may be inspired to skate like the children. Ice on my robe would refresh its fibers. Please lead us to the front table."

"This way, Mademoiselle. Be careful, the floor is slippery. You wouldn't want to fall and get your lovely ensemble wet and dirty." He said to himself, "I bet she and that ugly rag haven't seen soap and water since she escaped from the family farm."

Mary seated herself at the small table right next to the ice. She leaned forward touching the edge of the rink with her fingers.

"This is cool. Ice in the spring. Man, bet with your sweet words you can sell ice in the winter to the Eskimos."

"I do not understand why Eskimos surrounded by ice all year would want to buy ice from me when it is there for them free."

A group of waitresses stood motionless staring at the strange couple.

"Those kind never tip," said one.

The Buddha smiled at Mary, "But, my dear friend, I have seen a king with palace rooms filled with diamonds buy even more diamonds from traveling merchants. The king never even looked at his diamonds. Even his wives had no interest in their thick strands, weighing them down when they walked through town on special feast days. Perhaps Eskimos are like kings, both want more of what they already have. No one wants the new, the future, when he can just gather up more of the present."

"It's just a joke, man. You're too serious to get my tiny jokes. Let's order." She raised her arm at one waitress who had been whispering about them.

The waitress gave Mary a perfunctory nod.

"One giant-sized hot chocolate with lots and lots of whipped cream and an herbal tea for my friend. The whipped cream is the real stuff, isn't it?"

"Miss, it's so fresh, if you come down to the kitchen, I'll let you pet the cow."

Mary gave out a high-pitched giggle and the waitress immediately thawed, giving her a huge, welcoming smile.

"Great. At three bucks a cup, I don't want one of these spray job creams. I love hot chocolate super sweet." She sifted through the packets of sugar on the table. "I use that NutraSweet. It's made of pure chemicals. Don't use it with your tea. Try the real sugar. Tastes better, but it's not for me."

The Buddha said, "I am puzzled by her talk of cows. I know that in my country the poor farmers are pleased to share their houses with their cows, for some believe they are holy creatures. They can come and go as they please. They walk along the paths and stop in the fields to eat. When they return home at night, they are bathed and given water. Out of respect, the family will not eat their dinner until the cows come home. In this city of cars and lights, can the cows wander out in safety? How do they find food? Even your parks are crowded with people running in great pain and round discs flung through the air like shiny pebbles."

"Bud, you speak English perfect like a book or like a kid from some fancy prep school who never left the old estate. But they skipped the lesson on jokes. You are straight, man. You are really straight. I'll teach you about jokes and you can teach me about whatever. We got a deal?"

The Buddha nodded and read aloud from the menu, "Hot chocolate with whipped cream, hot chocolate plain, herbal tea, regular tea, decaffeinated espresso, cappuccino, decaffeinated cappuccino. All coffees and teas may be served either hot or iced."

He shook his head, "We do not have as many choices in my village. We have really just a few. We get milk from the cow and water from the river. The walls of our houses are bamboo or mud brick and all the roofs are made of branches from the palm tree. Necklaces for the young girls are made from tiny shells or small dried flowers. Does not too many choices focus you outward and wear down your hidden inside eye? In my country, when our hidden eye looks outward, we rejoice in seeing nothing to avoid entanglement in glittering surfaces."

The waitress returned and placed their drinks on the table.

Mary seemed to be in a trance, looking out over the ice. "Listen to that wonderful music," she said. "The Blue Danube. I last heard it as a kid." She moved her hand like a symphony conductor with a constant up and down to the beat and then, noticing her hot chocolate, took a long, slow sip.

"How's the tea? This hot chocolate is wonderful." She swished it around in her mouth and pushed her cheeks in and out to make the taste linger. She grabbed two more packs of the fake sugar and poured them into her mug. "Wanna hear about my last good hot chocolate?"

The Buddha had put down his teacup after two small sips and nodded to her.

"Well, my dad would drive me to our outdoor frozen basketball skating rink. Mom liked to stay home with the little kids. Funny, she hated the cold, though she grew up in southern Canada, which is higher north than Nebraska. Anyway, she'd take milk and melt chocolate—not that instant powder crap—and stir it in a black metal pot till it was smooth. Then when it was boiling, she'd quick empty it into my thermos bottle. I'd put a couple of teaspoons of sugar in the bottom when she wasn't looking. I loved that thermos. It had a huge red plastic cap that I could hardly get my hand around to screw it on and off. I loved sweets but I was thirsty all the time. Mom said I must be a camel 'cause I was always drinking water or fruit juice like I was going to cross the desert.

"My thermos was decorated with pictures of the Beatles. John was so wonderful. So cute. Each picture had an autograph and words streaming out of their mouths. 'I love you, yeah yeah yeah.' You don't get it?"

The Buddha shook his head.

"Oh, OK. These guys sang. How they sang! The Beatles, with an 'a', not insects like in your forests at home. Anyway, my dad would lift me up and drop me in the front seat of the old pickup. He'd wrap me in a huge green nylon sleeping bag 'cause the heater in the truck never worked for years. The truck would go bump, bump, over the dirt road frozen hard as concrete. I'd jiggle up and down like a tiny butterfly wiggling out of a green cocoon.

"We had a special game called Secrets. I'd tell my dad a secret and he'd tell me one. Hard to have secrets at home. See, I had to share a bedroom no bigger than a closet with my little sister and brother. Couldn't read at night 'cause Joey would cry to Mom that he couldn't sleep with the light burning in his eyes. Mom would yell and say, 'Read at school and turn off the light!' Couldn't whisper a little secret to Sissy, 'cause Joey would hear. But in the car, no one to hear. The wind would growl around us on the outside, so we were like in a space capsule hurtling to the moon. Know what secrets we told?"

"Please tell me your most wonderful secret. I will keep it a secret like a treasure hidden in an endless cave."

Mary waved her arm excitedly at the waitress. "That was great! Another cup, please. Go heavy on the whipped cream. Later we're going to the kitchen to pet the cow."

She plucked four more artificial sugar packets from the bowl. Two she dumped in her chocolate; two she tucked down her dress.

Secret Dream

"My most wonderful secret wasn't a real secret. It was a dream I kept having but I told it to my dad. You know, he had a secret dream but it was sort of real. Anyway, my dream always started out the same way. Say, do you believe in dreams?"

"Oh yes, my dear friend. After I sit quietly in one place, my mind becomes clear, not empty, but clear. Then stories rush into my head without my attention. These stories some call dreams."

"Good, real good. My dream always begins like this: I am a little girl. I mean I really was a little girl in real life. Anyway, I would be riding on a huge white horse with a coal black mane. We'd be going up a mountain that was almost in the clouds with snow so heavy all the pine trees were bending and swaying. I never hit the horse, just petted him on his neck and said, 'Faster, faster.' I had a sack of apples. We ate as we rode. I nibbled at them and the horse crunched them down in one bite. His name was Gemini. Do you know Gemini is an astrological sign? You believe in astrology?"

"Oh no. For if the exact second of our birth determines our entire life, how can we make mistakes? We need mistakes to overcome, to find our own way. We are not bees that can never make mistakes. Bees have marvelous patterns of flight that fake freedom. Bees could be controlled by an astrology sign."

"Well, in my secret dream, behind us on the path were eight or nine women running after us. They yelled, 'Stop, stop! We want to save you.' They were all waving huge black swords or short shiny knives that glistened off the light of the snow. As Gemini climbed up the trail, he stumbled on a moss-covered rock. I grabbed his mane to keep from sliding off his sweaty back. He slowed down and put down each hoof gently to test the muddy trail. The women were less than forty feet behind us. They weren't breathing hard, just gliding up the trail yelling, 'Let us save you! Let us save you!'

"We were only three hundred feet from the summit marked by huge granite boulders. I couldn't follow the trail because it narrowed as the boulders pressed together. Now I was really scared. I kept patting Gemini faster and faster with gentle strokes of my hand. He sprouted wings. His wings fluttered with a jerky motion so you could see them go up and down in little stops and starts. He flew like a pheasant, huffing about eight feet in the air almost surprised, looking down on the ground. Wanna hear about pheasants and my dad? That's a true story not part of my dream."

"Oh yes. Tell me about pheasants. That story you call true but dreams are also true."

"Well all this really happened. My dad would go out with his brother in the spring to hunt pheasants and he'd drag me along. I hated it but I liked to be with my dad. We'd wait hours and we weren't allowed to say a word, except in a whisper. Then, like firecrackers, their rifles would go off. The pheasants would twirl over and over as they fell.

"My dad would squeeze my hand and yell real loud, 'Got me one! Got me one!' He'd carry the bird back in the crook of his arm gentle-like. The long pretty tail feather he'd pull out and stick in my hair. 'Look real fancy now. Real fancy.'

"I felt sad for the bird but I smiled at my dad and said, 'Oh, Daddy. It makes me so beautiful. Real grown up.' Dad always tried to do nice things for me. Never seemed able to do much for me. For anyone. For himself. Never much at all. Not for a long time.

"Mom had to kill chickens every week. All year. She would smile when she'd come back to the kitchen. White plastic apron, streaked with fresh blood. She'd clean her ax with hot water, dry it carefully with a clean towel and sharpen it for next week.

"She wanted to teach me to kill the chickens. She'd say, 'If they're not killed, how you going to eat 'em? Chickens don't jump on your dinner plate by magic. That's how life is. How you going to feed yourself when you get bigger and no momma to take care of you?'

"She kept at me till I cried. 'So I won't eat chicken. I don't care.' I'd say. She'd yell at me and shriek, 'Then when I fix that goddamn bony pheasant one fancy dinner a year, don't eat that or I'll really fix you. Don't eat your father's lead-filled trophy.'

"Never ate pheasant either. Now I can talk about Mom later. I'll tell you about my dad's secret. He made his secret become real. Want to hear the rest of my dream now?"

"Yes, dear friend. Let your dream flow out," replied the Buddha.

"So, I had never seen a horse with wings except once in an old history book. I've seen lots of winged horses in bright red gas station signs, but never saw a live horse with wings.

"In my dream, the wings began to grow. The feathers of the wings became bright yellow, like gold. Then, a stream of little blobs of gold was flicking off from the end of each wing as it beat. The women became speckled with gold. They slowed down like a movie filmed in slow motion, their black hair turned golden. I couldn't hear their shouts. Then, their faces became covered with masks of gold like buried Inca princesses. They slowed and slowed, then they all stopped.

They were welded together—a chain of golden statues. Gemini struggled up the path, his wings hanging limp and pale.

"We were twenty feet from the summit. I just knew that on the other side of the mountain, there'd be a green valley with gentle rivers and sweet-smelling peach orchards. I'd be safe. I'd be in a new, lush country. Then it always happened, just before the top. Just when I could almost feel the warmth of the other side of the pass, I'd wake up. Every single time. I never saw the other side of the mountain. Never."

The Buddha said in a soft voice, "You never saw your secret promised valley. You never walked down its gentle paths. Yet you came close to the mountaintop."

"Oh sure, sure. Martin Luther King gave a speech that he reached the mountaintop, but he got killed. I was lucky I just woke up."

The Buddha held his teacup in both hands, moving it in a slow circle, watching the tea leaves swirl like a tiny whirlpool. He glanced up at the golden statue of Prometheus, forty feet in length, suspended over the bubbling pool of water. "Please, dear friend, tell me your dad's secret which was not a dream."

"My dad told me his secret when we were alone riding in his truck. He worked in a factory where they made stainless steel carts for hospitals or cheap metal carts for schools and sometimes even bent wires and aluminum tubing for supermarket carts. At the end of his shift, he'd pick up scraps of metal and put them in the back of his truck. He wasn't stealing. The factory paid some guy to pick up the leftovers and cart them away.

"In the corner of our barn, he had a workshop. Kept it locked all the time. Told Mom it was so no one would steal his tools while he was at work. His diamond blade saws could cut through metal thicker than a deck of cards. Ever seen acetylene torches make stainless steel run like butter? Wasn't true what he told Mom. He locked it so she couldn't come in and discover his secret.

"He loved to make stuff out of all his scraps. Little wondrous children or horses that I could hold in my hand like a baby. He made me a figure of a girl skating on one leg like a ballerina frozen in space by a flashbulb. Made it out of wire as thin as a hanger. The most special was a stainless steel horse small enough to fit in my hand. Hey, you know? It reminds me of Gemini, my dream horse! So beautiful. Two legs off the ground like a racehorse straining for the finish line.

"Late in the afternoon, I'd take it for a walk in the fields behind the shed. For a special treat, I'd let it stay out overnight all by itself. Of course, I'd leave a bowl of water and a couple of handfuls of hay so he had something to eat and sleep on. Always gleaming like silver. Nothing to rust or decay. I took it in my suitcase when I left home.

"What he liked best was to make metal sculptures two or three feet high out of circles and squares or long triangle pieces. When they were welded together, it was like magic. They soared. They were balanced, but when I'd walk around them they'd look different from every side. Never took anything he made out of his workshop. He'd tie them up to the rafters by thick ropes or stack 'em against the walls.

"I said, 'Please, please put a statue you made in the front yard.' Our neighbors had dopey painted wheelbarrows with flowers planted in 'em or a wooden Uncle Sam with red and white striped arms twirling in the wind.

"But Dad said Mom wouldn't like 'em. She'd call 'em junky, say he was wasting his time. He wouldn't even let me take my ballerina or horse into my room. I'd look at them on the shelf in a corner of his workshop or take them for a stroll when Mom was in town.

"Then one day he was practically dancing around with a folded newspaper in his hand. He opened it and read me the big headline that said, "Art Festival." He said they were having it about three hours away, and that he was going to bring his best sculpture to the show.

"He said, 'Maybe I'll win a prize, money or even a ribbon. I could become a real sculptor. Quit my lousy job after a while. Sell some statues. Hate to sell 'em though—they're my children. But I gotta sell 'em to feed my real children. To have a real studio with windows to look out and light coming in.'

"That was his secret—turning scraps of metal into beautiful, alive things. Made me swear on the Bible one Sunday when no one else was home that I'd never tell Mom. I swore never to say a word even if I was tortured and burned like Joan of Arc. I never did tell."

"Your father trusted you with his most precious secret: His dreams."

"Yeah, well anyway, I'll tell you the rest later. Wasn't I telling you about how my dad and I went skating?"

"Oh, yes. You went to skate on a frozen basketball rink, but a story should be finished like a statue, with all the vital pieces giving it shape. Please, continue."

"This round is on the house," chirped the waitress, as she approached them carrying a tiny silver tray with two cups emitting sweet clouds of steam. In one sweeping motion, she set down the new cups of hot chocolate and tea and cleared away the old ones.

"Say, did you know that Rockefeller Center has 175,000 visitors each day and 97,500 locks and 388 elevators which travel 1,984,000 miles a year up and down?" She paused as the Buddha shook his head. "Don't feel bad, Mister, most tourists don't know either. Hey, most Americans don't know. I only give this info to the foreigners, like I'm a guide, not just a robot carrying little trays."

Mary interrupted the waitress with a skinny-armed high five. "Great, the price for the drinks is right and 97,500 locks. Must be gold hidden in half the offices."

The Buddha smiled and held the steaming tea. He whispered to Mary, "Our waitress is gracious, though she speaks with words I understand and sentences that bewilder. Cows in the kitchen and now she speaks of a round and a house. I see nothing round. Our table is square. And a house! I see no house, only huge buildings surround us but there is no roof over our heads."

Mary laughed so hard that a few drops of chocolate spilled over the side of her cup as she held it overhead to toast the waitress. "You're funny, Bud. I'll buy you a book on slang next time I've got money to burn. You get that? Money to burn?"

The Buddha broke out in a big grin and raised his cup in imitation of Mary. "This is a toast for our waitress," he paused and added, "which she cannot eat. So please, continue your story."

State Fair: You a Full-Time Artist?

"My father asked Mom if she wanted to go to the state fair, but she said she didn't want to drive hours just to see oversized pigs or tomatoes that looked like volleyballs but tasted like pink sawdust or waste money on cotton candy that left you hungry and messy both.

"So she told my dad, 'Take the little princess, but don't waste more than two dollars on silly rides. Those stupid Ferris wheels are made for midgets. So you see more flat cornfields. No better than standing on a table. And those greasy bumper cars shake a kid's head till she throws up.'

"My dad tiptoed into my room and gave me a gentle pull on the shoulder. He was extra quiet so the other kids wouldn't wake up. It was real early, dark as night. Dad bent over and whispered in my ear, 'No blue jeans, kiddo. You're my princess. Prettiest girl at the state fair should wear her best dress.'

"He had made a huge bowl of thick oatmeal and a grown-up sized mug of hot chocolate. My lunchbox had two ham sandwiches and a couple of chocolate chip cookies. I stuffed in extra cookies so I wouldn't get hungry. I'd rather go up in the Ferris wheel than buy an old drowned-looking hot dog.

Dad must have gotten up at midnight 'cause the sculpture was already in the back of the truck, tied down under a canvas tarp that still showed specks of hay from protecting the pony's feed. On my seat in the truck, Dad had placed my favorite quilt with pictures of horses and wheat fields in its little squares. His mother had made it for me when I was born. The floorboards were covered with reddish soil and my legs dangled down, hovering over it.

"The ride was exciting. I get teased in New York, you know, 'What's to see in Nebraska? Flat as a pancake! No Niagara Falls, just little green cow ponds and scruffy trees!' This ride with my dad was so wonderful. Dad would look at a field with tiny plants growing in rows that stretched and stretched and say, 'Those are white corn, planted eight weeks ago. First crop. Ready for picking in five or six weeks, depending on the strength of the sun.' Then, in the hedges dividing the fields, he'd tell me the names of all the flowers. Little bluebells, crimson poppies, grand swaying Queen Anne's lace. He even stopped the truck and picked me a bouquet of all different flowers. Also, I think he took a pee, 'cause he stood real still with his back to me for a couple of minutes.

"When we got to the fair, it was so early, there was a rope strung in front of the entrance with a sign saying, 'Stop. No admittance to unauthorized persons.' Dad got out of the truck and walked over to a guy in a brown uniform sitting in his wooden booth. Dad clutched a big brown official-looking envelope that had been tucked in the visor along with old maps and discount coupons to McDonalds. The guard just sat there bored, not even curious about the big covered tarp bulging out from the back of the pickup. Then, like a magician pulling a scarf out of the air, Dad took out a carefully folded letter and handed it to the guard.

"He sort of grunted out, 'Straight ahead till you come to the giant tomatoes and take a left. Keep going straight. Can't miss the monster tent at the end. Big art exhibition banner in front.' Then he got out and pulled aside the rope and made a little bow. 'Good luck, Mister, with whatever you're hiding under that canvas. Hope it's a statue of a naked woman and not another smiling child with lots of teeth holding a bunch of flowers. Seen three of those already.'

"Boy, was I proud of my dad. We went in like open sesame. Even the dumb guard knew my dad was an artist with an official letter. I gave him a little red poppy from my bouquet and said, 'Stick it through your buttonhole for luck.'

"We drove up to the main tent and backed the truck around where it said, 'Art Exhibitors Unloading Only.' My dad pulled me down from the cab. He was smiling and started to walk real straight-backed like a marine on parade. Inside, there was a man dressed up in a dark blue suit with a badge proclaiming, 'Head of Art Exhibition.' He motioned to two young men with a lot of muscles in tight t-shirts who went with my dad to carry in the statue. 'Don't want any harm to that statue getting it unloaded. Looked real good in the photos. Ever show your work before, sir?' I'd never heard anyone call my dad 'sir.' He had his hands hidden in his pockets and his arms were close against his sides. With a nod so small I barely saw it, he said, 'This is the first time anyone except my little girl here has seen what I do.'

"'Well, good luck. Don't be disappointed if you don't win a prize. Over a hundred artists are competing. Some real good, full-time artists. You a full-time artist?'

"My father looked down at the ground. 'No, real part-time. Work in a factory and farm little pigs, corn, chickens. I love it, but never enough time. Never.'

"'Sent you the rules, didn't we? We judge today and give out the prizes tonight at seven sharp. Everyone can pick up their work when the fair is over in two weeks. Take your girl around the fair. Here's a pass. All the rides are free for both of you today. See you later.'

"This pass was a magic wand. Wave it and get in free. Free! I could save the coins in my pocket for cotton candy. We went up in the Ferris wheel eight times in a row. Dad would just show the pass and the guy would pull this long wooden lever and we'd start up again. I said, 'Wish Mom could see us now. She'd be proud even if you don't win a prize.'

"Dad didn't say anything for two or three rides, but looked straight out at the flat fields of corn surrounding the fairgrounds like some green and brown striped ocean.

"The next time we were swaying at the top, my dad said, 'When we're so high, the earth looks smaller. People look like ants. You look so grown-up to me. Big and grown-up sitting right next to me. Being up here you get a new way of looking at things. See that highway down there? That little ribbon leads all the way to New York. Looks like a tiny stream with a swift current. Always pulling. Always pulling away. Never been to New York. That's where real artists live. Ever hear of Greenwich Village? Streets crowded with artists and cafes.'

"He paused and looked away. Over the metallic clank of the Ferris wheel ratcheting down gear by gear, he whispered, 'Your dad will always love you. We can share lots of secrets together, even if we're not sitting close.'

"The fire engine red loudspeakers were strung up like Christmas lights on telephone poles all over. Someone with a real farm twang sounding out of breath boomed over the speakers, 'Hurry over to the cattle judging. These cows are champions. Hurry on over folks. Nothing to pay. Which of your neighbors will win the blue ribbon? Hurry on over. Judge for yourself.'

"Around dinnertime, when I was so stuffed with hot dogs and cotton candy washed down by Cokes that I sort of waddled, I heard this announcement, 'Art exhibition prizes announced in fifteen minutes. Cash prizes. See who will be our own Michelangelo. Hurry on over. Judge for yourself.'

"I grabbed my dad's hand and pulled him toward the big tent. His face was kind of blank, like he wasn't interested. And he just let me drag him by the hand like I was the grown-up. His hand was sweaty and he kept licking his lips. We sat down in the front row on those wooden chairs that fold up. Must have been two hundred people milling around or twisting around on those creaky chairs.

"At the back of the tent, there was a pile of chairs six feet high with their bottoms all stenciled, 'Property of AAA Rental.' When someone came in the tent, a kid in a brown uniform with arms like an ape would swoop up a chair, snap it open with a bang, stick it like an oversized door prize in the person's face and say, 'Carry it wherever you want to sit. Judging about to start. Get a good seat.'

"The stage was an unpainted wooden platform three feet off the ground. Dad just sat there staring at it. On the front of the podium there was a silky banner of the official state seal. On one side of the stage, the flag of Nebraska was kind of limp against its flagpole. At the other side, Old Glory was waving gently in the hot air humming out of a small fan. There was so much cigarette smoke that it hurt when I stretched my eyes to see everything.

"After about ten minutes, a dozen people in the back started this rhythmic clapping. Soon the whole place was clapping louder and louder, like a revival meeting just before the preacher does the first miracle. A little man with a white shirt and sky-blue tie marched up on the platform and raised both his hands not to give a blessing, but to tell everyone to sit down and be quiet. Dad and I were so quiet. He never said a word, but held both my hands real tight in his big fist.

"Well, Mister Blue Tie welcomed all of us then stretched an arm toward five people huddled at the base of the stage. 'Ladies and gentlemen, let's welcome our distinguished judges from the Fine Arts Department of University of Nebraska.' He started to clap real hard with his arms moving so fast they began to blur.

"The audience gave a few claps back but this gang in the back started to chant, 'Who won? Who won?'

"So Mister Blue Tie raised his hands again, this time like a surrender in a war movie. 'In these envelopes, I have the decisions of our judges who are either artists of some fame or have devoted their lives to analyzing twentieth century American and European art. All the entrants get an honorable mention ribbon and a certificate suitable for framing.'

"Then, he took a big breath and said, ' Now for the winners: Third prize of one hundred dollars to Joanie Speller, an art major at UK, for her lovely oil painting of wheat fields at sunset.' He clapped again as this woman dressed in black jeans and a black t-shirt walked up to the stage. The picture was carried up and placed on an easel, and one of the judges pinned a ribbon on the frame.

"The group in the back whistled and stomped, 'Our Joanie did it! Go, Joanie, go!'

"A tall thin woman with glasses turned to a man who was writing something down on a clipboard and said, 'Bet she was inspired by the dairy farmer's calendar.'

"Joanie Speller shook Blue Tie's hand, tore open the envelope, kissed the check and waved it at the crowd.

"My dad leaned over to me and whispered, 'Bet she's seen pictures of Greenwich Village and never been east of Chicago.'

"Mister Blue Tie coughed into the mike two or three times. 'The second prize of three hundred dollars is awarded to Daniel Harp who teaches sculpture at Omaha Community College. His bronze statue is entitled, *Girl with Flowers*.' Blue Tie began to clap slightly harder than his third-prize clap as a man with a big head of white hair and a red beard ambled up on the stage. He took his prize, clasped his hands over his bulky frame and trotted down to the seat next to Joanie Speller.

"The thin woman with glasses nudged her companion who was still writing feverishly, 'Certainly must pull the creative juices out of his pupils if they have brown sugar for blood. That little bronze girl is so sweet I could vomit. Really daring and creative. Pushing back the frontiers of art in our fair state! Bet these distinguished judges save the shmaltziest for last. Know what schmaltz is? Chicken fat. Pure unadulterated chicken fat.'

"'And now, ladies and gentlemen,' Blue Tie continued, 'what we have all been waiting for: The grand prize.' He nodded his head and the lights strung along the rafters inside the tent went off. A single spotlight illuminated the podium. It switched from red to blue to white, making a colorful cloud of the smoke in the tent. Two brawny stagehands placed a big red velvet covered statue in the middle of the stage.

"Blue Tie made a few staccato coughs and began, 'Now for the Grand Prize and five hundred dollars—The committee is pleased to announce that the Grand Prize winner has never exhibited anywhere. We are also pleased that he chose us and we chose him. I am sure this exceptionally talented artist will have a wonderful future.' Then, he whipped the velvet cover off and there was my dad's sculpture!

"I tore my hands out of Dad's grasp and gave him a giant hug. Dad wiped his eyes with the back of his hand. My head was pressed into his chest. It was hard to hear the thump thump of his heart. It usually sounded like a strong bellows to me.

"'Dad, you won! You won! My dad is a real artist!' I screamed. I gave him a big kiss on his cheek.

"The woman with glasses gave me a quizzical look as she started to walk toward the stage with her assistant who had now unsheathed a huge camera with a flashbulb attachment as big as a basketball. 'On behalf of all the judges and the Nebraska State Committee on the Arts and the Nebraska State Fair, I am pleased to announce that the winner is a man who works during the day in a factory, farms in the afternoon and works on his art in the evenings and on weekends. The prize is for his steel and aluminum sculpture called, *Winged Flight*. Let's give a big hand to Dan Forest.'

"Blue Tie began to clap. The audience rose in unison with bursts of noisy clapping and shouts from the back, 'Way to go, Jim baby!'

"Dad stood up and took a step toward the stage. He turned around, and said, 'Come on, princess. You helped me get here.'

"As Dad shook hands with Blue Tie in front of the statue, the woman with glasses said, 'Move to the left so the readers will see it. Tell the little girl to stand in front on the other side. Nice human interest touch.'

"She turned to her assistant and told him, 'Take half a dozen shots. Get one good one. I know your photographic batting average.' Then, to us she said, 'Smile, folks. Look natural!'

"After the flashbulbs were finished, she walked over to Dad. She held a mike from a tape recorder she had slung over her shoulder like a metal purse and gushed, 'Congratulations, Mr. Forest. How long have you been doing sculpture? Who taught you?'

"Dad licked his lips. He clutched the check with one hand and me with the other. 'Well, nearly six years. Part-time. Real part-time. Just started…Bent scraps of metal to make toys for my little girl here, you know, little animals or an angel with tiny wings.'

"'So, will you devote more time to your work now?'

"'Yeah, only if my little girl approves. Artists can be lonely, really alone. Cut off.'

"The woman bent over and stuck her mike about an inch from my face, 'Do you approve, young lady?'

"My tongue swelled up in my mouth so I could hardly breathe. I blew all the air out of my mouth like wishing on birthday candles. 'My dad is a real artist. Course I approve! I love him. We have secrets together. He will never be alone.'

"Turning to Dad, she said, 'I'll send you a dozen copies of the article. Your work is exciting. Keep it up. You have a wonderful little fan here too.'

"Dad looked a little troubled. He hesitated and said, 'Please send the copies to me at my factory. It's easier that way.'

"I guessed Dad was so proud. First prize! Maybe he'd get famous. All his buddies at the factory would be impressed big-time. No more teasing him for looking dreamy or asking him why he put tiny scraps of metal in his work overalls.

"'Can we ride more on the Ferris wheel? Let's call Mom. I saved some change. Bet she'll be surprised. Maybe she'll make us a fancy dinner.'

"Dad gave me a big grin. 'No, let's wait. I'll tell her tomorrow when she wakes up. Sure, let's ride late as you want. You can sleep in the truck. It's nice to drive late at night, like it's your own private road. Just crickets bleating out. No birds chirping—they're all asleep in tiny hidden nests.'

"Dad carried me to the truck like a sack of potatoes. With all the cotton candy and French fries in me, I felt like a bloated sack hiding out in a party dress. The next morning, as I lay in bed thinking about the magic wand pass and all the rides free for a day, I heard Mom's voice so loud and angry I thought maybe the barn had burned down and barbecued all the pigs.

"'So you're a five hundred dollar big shot with a picture of you and princess in the newspaper!? How much money you spend on fancy tools hidden in your secret art studio? How much?'

"Through the wall, I heard Dad walking hard, up and down on the squeaking wooden floor like he was stomping his boots in anger.

"Mom's voice had a harsh fake syrupy quality, so sweet you choke in anger. 'Win three grand prizes like that and you'll be bringing in ten cents an hour. Wetbacks make more. I slave for three kids. Never time for me and you're an artist. Thanks for all your precious help. Maybe the union could let me take your job at the factory. I'd bring home overtime. You could stay here seven wonderful days a week!'

"The front door slammed so hard the little plastic cross on my nightstand fell off. It didn't break. Mom must have been yelling out the open doorway, I could barely hear her with the wind coming in. Sounded like, 'Big-shot artist!'

"The wind blew the black smell of burning pancakes into my room. I got dressed in my other good dress, ready for Sunday church.

"Mom pretended nothing had happened. She said, 'Pancakes burned. Make yourself toast. Church in ten minutes.'

"Dad pulled up the truck without opening the door. Mom pulled it open and we all climbed in. She slammed the door so hard, my dress nearly got caught.

"Dad stared at the road and was silent. On the way to church, he'd usually say, 'That dress is so nice,' or 'Your hair is lovely with that big bow.' He said nothing the whole way to church and nothing the whole way back. Say, you know why I love hot chocolate?"

"There are many sweet drinks but favorites always come with a dream or a story," replied the Buddha.

"This is all true. Every single word. We used to go ice-skating and drink hot chocolate. When we'd go skating, my dad always brought kindling, two unbent metal hangers and big thick coffee mugs decorated with valentine hearts.

"Wrapped in the sleeping bag like some Indian chief, he'd watch me go round and round on the ice. When I slowed down, he'd start a fire. He'd let me tear open the tiny box of Campfire marshmallows and spear them on the wire stick. When they were brown and crispy, I'd suck off the skin and drop the warm white center blob into the mugs filled with steaming chocolate. I'd sip very slowly so the sweet blob could shrink as I reached the bottom.

"But even better than chocolate was when my dad put on his old-fashioned black ice skates and we'd skate around, holding hands. I felt like a queen or maybe a princess. No other girl ever came to the rink and skated with her dad. The other girls just got dropped off and left there.

"I also learned to sorta fly. My dad would hold each of my hands and start to twirl around. As he spun faster and faster, I'd lift my legs off the ice and go round him like a propeller on a Piper Cub two feet off the ground.

"I begged him to have Mom come one time and watch me fly. At first he said, 'She's too busy,' or 'Who'll watch the babies?' Maybe he didn't want her to come to our special place. But every time we came home from skating, I told her Dad and me had a special surprise to show her when she'd come.

"By the end of the season, I'd worn her down. So one day she bundled herself into the truck saying, 'This better be worth it. Paying to have the babies sat with!' Dad brought another cup and a third unbent hanger, but Mom didn't drink chocolate 'cause she said it uglied up her skin.

"When we got there, Mom sat in the sleeping bag, not looking too interested. She was just waiting for my surprise. When she saw me start to fly, she jumped out from the bag and ran over to us shouting at my dad, 'Damn fool, stop right now! Stop! Stop! Want her to break her head open or spear a kid with her skates when you slip, you dumb no-good oaf?'

"My dad stared at her hard-like and moved his mouth but no words came out.

"She told us to throw ice on the fire. We were leaving. I started to cry so loudly, my chest hurt. Dad picked me up in his big arms and carried me to the truck, skates and all. There wasn't a word spoken the whole ride home. I took off my skates. That was the last time I ever had skates on my feet."

The Buddha replied, "My dear friend, you led me to this skating rink nestled in the soft air of spring. Skating is dangerous as your mother said long ago. Danger comes to those who rush forward and to those who stand motionless. When a rock roars down a hill, it strikes without a careful plan. Yet, to curse a kind father in front of his child harms all three. The father will cease to teach; the daughter will cease to learn; the mother will cease to receive their double love."

Mary stood up, hot chocolate in hand. She raised the cup in a gracious toast to the Buddha. "You make me wanna put on skates and try my rusty legs. Bet they didn't forget their bends and sweeps." She drained the cup like it was fine champagne.

She stood up and said to the Buddha, "Stay here. Don't pay. Order more tea. As the general said, 'I shall return.' You know, you were right on about my mom and dad. They finally split. Life gets screwed up not because of your big philosophical tragedies, but all the little messes. I'll tell you that story later." She gave the Buddha a thumbs-up salute as she sauntered to the skate rental window.

The waitress approached the Buddha. "Need a refill? It's on the house." The Buddha looked puzzled. "I mean free and complimentary. No charge. Get it?"

"I thank you my friend. Why do you conceal the grains of tea in such a tiny sack? At home we pour it in, we wait, we watch it settle in a gently lowering spiral. It becomes part of the water and gives off little colored streams. When we drink it, the grains are carried upward. They allow themselves to be chewed so our tongues can feel their essence."

"Yuck!" the waitress grinned. "Those little seeds floating around and sticking between your teeth? I'd sell about a cup a month. But if that's what you like, sorta like home-style, I can tear the sack open and shake it over the cup. You want essence? We give you essence."

Mary appeared at the other side of the rink. She gave the Buddha a vigorous wave. "Hey, old buddy! Look at the kid now." She put one skate forward, tapping tentatively as if she were afraid the ice would break under her weight and swallow her. She took half a dozen jerky small steps. "No pain, no gain. No glide, no slide. I'll get there, just keep watching," she uttered to herself. She pushed off with one leg, then bent her knees and threw her arms back like a downhill skier. The momentum took her to the end of the rink. "Look at me! Even the Wright brothers didn't go too far on their first flight. It's coming back to me. I'm going to fly again!"

The waitress returned to the Buddha's table and with a slow, exaggerated gesture, tore the teabag in two and let the seeds drop into the cup of steaming water. "Chew on the seeds to your heart's content."

"I will. Thank you for preparing my tea home-style."

"No problem." She gave Mary a big thumbs-up salute and turning back to the Buddha, she said, "Your friend looks scared, but acts brave. Know what this thumbs-up means?"

"I do, for I have traveled in history. In Rome, the crowds would give thumbs-up or thumbs-down to decide the fate of gladiators and Christians."

"So, you're a history buff," the waitress exclaimed. "In this country, we didn't kill Christians because we're all still mainly Christians, but we did love to kill witches. If the witches confessed they were witches, then they were burned, for witches must be burned. If the woman did not confess, she was burned for lying—too dishonest to say she was a witch."

"In my country, we do not even have a word like 'witch.' Perhaps our mother tongue is primitive."

"Mister, you come from a very boring part of the world. Do you know what we have? We have witches, devils, demons, monsters, ghosts, ghouls, werewolves and harpies. I could go on like a little thesaurus, but you get the idea, don't you?"

"Oh yes, my friend. In my country, we lack monsters. So, without monsters, we must also do without gods, for the two are entwined, if not inseparable, just like Siamese twins that cannot live apart. Look at my friend, she is not flying, but she begins to move with the grace of the young girl she was."

Mary wove in and out through the skaters as if she were a happy thread in a human tapestry. She stopped as she passed a man in the center of the rink twirling his little daughter by her hands. Her legs and body had floated up from the ice.

The man began to spin faster and faster, cutting a small tight pattern in the ice. The child shrieked in a terrified laughter, "Faster, Daddy, faster! Make me fly to the moon!" The little child was a blur of white leggings and bright pink sweater. "Faster! Faster!"

The man strained to increase his speed. His face became red with a fixed grimace. He raised his arms higher and higher until they were over his head and the child was like a leaf in a whirlwind.

The Buddha saw the man start to stumble as his skates became entangled. The man strained to lean backward in the other direction just as a sailor leans from the high side of the deck in an effort to pull his sailboat to a more even keel. He instinctively stretched out one hand to cushion his fall. As he fell to the ice, he released his grip on his daughter. His child, freed from gravity, soared in a gentle arc, feet first toward an infant on a ringside table strapped into a pink plastic portable car seat.

The other skaters yelled, "Look out! Get away! Skates will slash!" Mary stood still for an instant as if hypnotized. Then she made a deliberate turn like a matador facing the horns of an enraged bull. She snapped her arms around the waist of the screaming girl, grabbing her before she reached the infant. The momentum of the child knocked Mary backward as though she had caught a spear in midair.

The Buddha had risen from his chair and was running toward them as he saw Mary's head hit the ice. The little girl fell on top of Mary who lay on her back with her arms and legs spread out in the form of a giant X. The Buddha kneeled beside her. She was laying still.

The waitress ran out onto the ice, dropped to her knees and put her head lightly against Mary's chest. Then she felt for a pulse from the limp wrist.

The waltz music had stopped. The man whose daughter Mary had caught in mid-air had risen from the ice and taken his child in his arms. He tried to comfort her, but she was convulsed with tears. He rocked her slowly back and forth. He began to sob as he looked down at Mary, unconscious on the ice. "Did I kill her? Oh God almighty."

His wife bolted out of her ringside table and ran toward them screaming out in a harsh voice, "You showoff! You fool! You made our child a loose missile. You coulda killed her! You killed that woman that saved her. Get an ambulance."

The other skaters formed a silent chorus around the rink. The waitress walked out to the center of the ice and announced in a booming, authoritative voice, "Folks, we called 911. The emergency medical team will arrive in a couple of minutes. So please, clear the ice now. Sit down. This young lady will be fine. Just please clear the ice for the medics."

She whispered to the Buddha, "Mister, make sure you go with her to the hospital. It'll be OK." She paused. "No. Listen, I got an idea. Those hospital folks will take one look at you and throw you out. I'll go with you and say I'm her sister and you're my friend. What's her name?"

"Her name is Mary."

"OK listen, my name is Liz Starr. We'll tell them her name is Mary Starr. What's your name?

"You can call me Bud."

"Great name. This Bud's for you. Bet you don't even drink. We got our story set. Here come the medics. I'll tell 'em you're my boyfriend. We're going to the biggest emergency hospital in the world. Ever see ER on TV?"

"No, we don't have emergency rooms in my country. We have emergencies and carry the hurt one to the nearest hut, call the family and run to find the village elder trained in healing. But look, has she opened her eyes?"

Liz had seen no movement in Mary's eyes and shook her head as she gave the Buddha a comforting pat on his robed arm. The Buddha's face had lost its composed look. His eyes no longer sparkled. The ends of his lips had sunk downward, giving him a somber expression.

Emergency Medical Team: Velcro Straps Around Her Chin

Two emergency medics arrived and moved rapidly across the ice to Mary. They were twin brothers with shoulder-length hair and identical white jumpsuits. They both supported huge backpacks on their tight muscular frames and held one end of the six-foot-long rigid backboard.

Leonard had a large oxygen tank strapped on top of his pack and looked like a scuba diver out of water. His twin, Dave, set down a bulky-looking briefcase on the ice, and opened it to reveal a TV-like screen. They gently lifted Mary and placed her on the backboard.

Dave put a cervical collar around her head. Then, with a minimum of movement, they placed Velcro straps around her chin and over her forehead to keep her head from moving. With additional straps around her lower body, she was completely immobilized.

Dave placed his stethoscope on Mary's chest and closed up his TV briefcase. He put his hand on her wrist to feel her pulse. Pushing up her eyelid, he saw a large diluted pupil staring out. Leonard then covered her with a thick gray blanket so just her head stuck out.

He pulled out what looked like a portable phone and began speaking, "OK, ER, our ETA is twelve minutes even with the cops. But I'll be there in ten. Gotta be there in ten. Cops will escort. Looks like big-time coma. Head hit ice. Yeah, ice I said. I-C-E. Some head bleed. Yeah, I know if we don't make it in ten minutes, she might never...Check. Check. Yeah, check."

As Liz approached Dave, she rubbed her hand over her eyes as if she were wiping away tears. "She's my sister. Back of her head cracked into the ice. Take us with you. Me and my boyfriend here. Oh God, poor sis. She'll be OK?"

"OK, you're family, but your boyfriend?"

"Don't worry. I'll sit on his lap. He'll keep me calm."

"Get in the front. No time to argue. We got nine minutes."

The Police Arrive: I'll Clear the Crowd

Two motorcycle policemen had ridden up the walkway overlooking the rink and stopped next to the EMS ambulance. The taller cop ran down the stairs to the rink while the other guarded the two cycles with their humming engines and blinking red warning lights. The cop bristled with high-tech efficiency as he bounded down the stairs two at a time. Around his waist, he had a walkie-talkie, a glistening service revolver in a black leather gun belt and a small handheld computer scanner with an electric cord that ran to a hidden battery under his jacket.

"Hey, Dave!" the cop yelled. "Need a hand? Ready to roll? We'll get Fifth Ave. cleared by the time you're in the ambulance." He gave a quick glance at Mary from behind his silver aviator glasses and said, "I'll clear the crowd, mount the cycle, juice up the old siren. I'll lead the triumphal procession to the ER and leave."

"Yeah, Tim, lead and leave. The motto of New York's finest. Grab our packs. This damned ice is slippery. Gotta be careful moving across it. In my next life, I'll wear shades, carry a big gun strapped to the old belly and get respect. OK. One. Two.

Three. Slow lift." The two medics raised Mary and moved across the ice with precise steps like marines at a parade.

Liz puffed as she jogged up the stairs. "Gotta quit smoking," she announced to no one in particular. She looked at the Buddha who had pulled his robe nearly up to his knees as he marched up the stairs. "Sandals? How can you wear sandals in this filthy city. The dog shit will eat away your toes."

The Buddha knew that in his country everyone wore sandals except beggars and children who went barefoot. The dung of the elephants attracted the youngest children who would stand on the hardened crust and dare heavier older ones to find a similar spot. When a bigger child's foot plunged through the surface, there were peals of laughter. If adults were nearby, they would put the droppings in bags of woven hemp and carry them to the fields.

The Buddha had never seen anyone's toes eaten away. Perhaps, he mused, city dogs are so mean and angry that they like to harm their masters, while elephants help their masters grow the rice that feeds everyone.

A growing crowd lined the stairs. A white-haired tourist wearing a Statue of Liberty baseball cap was standing on tiptoes so that he could see all the action. As the procession neared, he yelled, "Chester, get the video camera. Look at that cool cop!"

A couple of young New Yorkers stood silently, trying to appear uninterested, but stared in unison at the trickle of blood oozing from Mary's head.

Liz smacked a young man in a cowboy shirt and tight jeans who had aimed his video camera a foot from her face. The camera clattered to the stone stairs. The lens shattered and the whir of tapes became an irregular click. The young man yelled, "You broke my camera. I'm getting a cop."

Liz paused, raised her hand with one finger pointing skyward and said, "My sister's dying. Call the whole damn police force." She threw a few coins at his face. "Take this. Buy a throwaway camera. Get lost. You want a freak show? Stand in front of a mirror and slit your ugly throat."

The cop stepped between the two and poked the man gently on the chest with his billy stick. "Now Mister, just move on or you'll get a free ride in the paddy wagon for interfering with medics and New York City police officers in an emergency. Take the lady's coins, pick up that camera and move! Now! We got seven frigging minutes to get to the ER."

The Race Down Fifth Avenue: Sirens Wail Like Hungry Children

The procession reached the back of the ambulance. The two back doors were wide open and a black metal ramp led to the inside. Orange lights flashed in the back and the irregular wail of the siren rose and fell every few seconds. Three more cops on motorcycles were waiting in front of the ambulance, seated like statues. Occasionally, like a chorus line, they would jam their feet down on the accelerators causing puffs of white smoke to emerge in deafening staccato bursts of angry sound.

The medics moved up the ramp into the ambulance and pulled the back doors shut. The Buddha and Liz squeezed into the passenger seat, while Dave jumped in and started the engine. The crowd moved backward as the engine was revved up.

The cop's voice boomed over the sirens and honking of motorists who were jammed on Fifth Avenue, "Show's over, folks. Keep moving."

In the back of the ambulance, Leonard had locked the backboard in place and then strapped Mary down. A thick block of rubber with a scooped-out center now further cushioned her head.

"You won't even feel this," Leonard said as he plunged an IV drip into Mary's left arm. Then with great care, he applied a pressurized bandage to stem the blood flowing from her scalp. Her eyes were closed and her breathing was short and rapid.

"Now, take a good deep breath. That's it. Fine. Real fine." He had placed a cupped plastic oxygen mask over her nose and mouth. "Just stay calm. Be there in a sec. Nine minutes or bust." Mary's eyes stayed shut, but her breathing became slow and regular. The medic unrolled a pair of blue plastic trousers, pulled them up over Mary's legs and pushed the lever on a small gas canister causing the trousers to expand like inner tubes.

Leonard called up to Dave, "Dressed her in the MASTs. Pulse down to fifty."

"What's a mast? You guys sailors?" Liz asked.

Dave replied, "That means medical anti-shock trousers. Keeps the blood from going down into the legs. Keeps it up in the head and heart where she needs it. Just look out the window. Ever been escorted down Fifth by motorcycle cops?"

"Sure, whenever my cousin, the Queen of England, comes, I tootle around in the royal limo. She gives me port in real crystal. The president's limo has cheap bourbon and so crowded, with the Secret Service hunks—no class at all."

The Buddha squeezed toward the window away from Liz.

"Hey Mister, eh, Bud, just relax. I gotta press my butt somewhere so Dave here can play at racecar driver. Right, Dave?"

"Just listen to the music and chill out. This is a race against…never mind, just chill out," Dave said without looking at the strange couple to his right.

The Buddha heard no music, merely a soft rhythm from the back of the ambulance and the honking horns of cars blocked on the side streets emptying into Fifth Avenue. "The sirens from the motorcycles wail like hungry children, but multiplied a hundred times. Have you ever heard children cry for milk?" the Buddha asked Liz.

"My little sister would cry for about five seconds and my grandmother would make me run to the fridge for a bottle. See, I was the oldest kid and Mom and Dad were always out working. Got to hold the baby and stick the bottle in her mouth. Shut her up quick. But if there was no bottle, the baby would cry and Grandma would yell bloody murder. Why didn't I keep a bottle in the fridge ready like she told me? You gotta blame someone when a baby screams."

"In my country," the Buddha explained, "milk could not be kept cool in huts or even in the palace. But since the cow lived but a few steps away or on the other side of the wall, we kept the milk in its natural container. When a baby started to wail, the next oldest would give it a piece of sugarcane to suck on. A larger child would run to a cow and pull until warm steaming milk filled the cup. No one blames a cow who does not give milk anytime day or night. There is always another cow or the cow of a neighbor. The baby would smile while it sucked the sweet juice of the sugarcane. Why should a mother scream when a baby is smiling?"

Dave had been following the motorcycle cops down Fifth Avenue. "Watch 'em part the cars to each side. Make 'em scrunch toward the sidewalk. Remember the movie where Moses parted the Red Sea to escape? Boy, were the Egyptians pissed. Bet their descendants drive half the cabs the cops just forced to pull over. Just as pissed, too. Let 'em honk. Wave their fists. Let 'em go home and drive a camel—Oh my God." Dave put on the brakes as gently as he could to avoid a large bus that had pulled out from the curb and sideswiped a cab. Both drivers had jumped out. Dave rolled down the window to yell, but the two drivers were now pushing each other.

The path the cops had cleared was now a narrow gap to the left between the dented cab and a large newspaper delivery truck that had pulled within a few feet of the curb.

"Five minutes to D-day and I gotta thread a needle," Dave muttered.

"You know, Bud," Liz said, "we are truly honored to be with Dave here. He saves lives like a doctor, drives like a pro at the Indy 500 and drops tidbits from epic movies—*The Ten Commandments* in living color. Plus, little pearls of sociology cast before swine. A man for all seasons."

Emergency Room: Ok, Let's Go

The motorcycles slowed down at Fifth Avenue and Thirty-fourth Street so that the ambulance could make a left turn without being rammed in the intersection.

"How's the breathing back there?" Dave asked.

"Getting weaker and shallower. Gotta get us there in four minutes. Pulse is slowing. Juice the old gas pedal."

What happens after four minutes, Dave?" Liz asked with a false calmness in her voice.

"Well, you see, that's our ETA—estimated time of arrival. We just like to be on time. Prompt. It's nothing. Don't worry." Dave looked straight ahead. His hands squeezed the steering wheel so hard they turned white.

"Well," Liz replied, "if four minutes doesn't mean anything, why worry that the countdown is three now?" She glanced at her plastic watch. "See, this watch cost me two dollars on the street, but it's great. Click the button and like magic, a stopwatch with a countdown function. All for two dollars. No sales tax."

Liz craned her neck toward the window. "Look straight

up, Bud. It's the Empire State Building. Tallest building in the world. One hundred and three stories."

As the ambulance whizzed by, the Buddha glanced at the skyscraper. He said to Liz, "The Empire building looks no taller than its neighbors. If you are so close to greatness, the greatness may escape your eyes. When you have traveled far away, it is much easier to recognize greatness, for it stands out."

The ambulance sped by the front of the old Bellevue emergency room. The building was classic yellow-orange brick with a squat section of a roman column marking the entrance. The massive windows on the first floor had cheerful children's paintings of animals and beaches. The former garden was strewn with six-foot-high massive chunks of roman columns unceremoniously dumped as if upended by a tornado.

The Buddha saw men seated on the ground in small groups drinking from a brown paper bag. Two men had rushed out into the street, chasing a bottle that was rolling in front of them. "Christ, Dave. Honk. Hit 'em. The watch says fifty seconds," Liz advised.

Dave gave the ambulance a sharp turn and pulled up onto the pockmarked concrete sidewalk, just missing one of the drunks holding his bottle up like an Olympic gold medal.

The ambulance came to a smooth stop in front of the new emergency room entrance. A gleaming stainless steel slab stuck out at a right angle from the flat facade, protecting the entry from the elements.

Dave ran over to two orderlies waiting with a stretcher. "OK, lets go." He opened the back doors of the ambulance. They moved Mary's canvas stretcher with measured steps toward the hospital stretcher as Leonard emerged crab-like from the ambulance.

Mary's eyes were shut and her shallow breathing caused Dave to frown. Her legs were encased in the inflated plastic trousers so that she looked half like the rotund tire man and half like a young schoolgirl.

"Hit her head about eighteen minutes ago. Dripped two hundred cc's of saline. Pulse sixty over palp. Heartbeat steady. Applied compression bandages," Dave recited.

Liz clicked her stopwatch, "What was the rush? Fourteen seconds to spare. We won!"

Dave's deadpan response was simply, "Yeah, it's good to win. There's no second prize. And no second chance."

The Hospital: The Waiting Room

The Buddha and Liz watched Mary disappear in a crowd of green gowns, white jackets, four IV bottles and two machines with little television monitors.

A dark-skinned, white-jacketed man standing next to Mary's stretcher called out in a British accent, "Hurry along, mates. There's a big reception waiting up in surgery as soon as we do a CAT scan. Lead the way to the elevator, damn bloody fools!"

For an instant, the crowd parted and the Buddha saw Mary's still face with a thin tube stuck in her nose and a thick one going down her mouth. Then he saw them wheel Mary's gurney into a doublewide elevator.

"Sit down. Make yourself comfortable if you can. You'll get some word from the big medical cheeses in thirty minutes," Dave explained.

The waiting room was separated from the emergency room by beige plastic dividers about three feet high. A tall security guard sat like a toll taker at the entrance to the ER to keep visitors from rushing in to comfort a groaning or unconscious patient. Plastic chairs were all bolted to the floor in a straight line. Armrests stuck out between each chair, not for comfort, but like in an airport lounge in a third-world country, so no one could stretch out and sleep.

Liz walked back and forth like a soldier on guard duty. "Damn," she cried, "Bud, I'm going outside for a quick puff. Makes me feel like a criminal doing drugs hanging around in smelly doorways. Just need a lousy cigarette. I'll be back."

The rows of chairs in the waiting area looked directly toward the large surrounding stage of the emergency room like the orchestra seats in a theater. The Buddha sat at the end of the back row. He tucked his feet up on the seat and smoothed out his robe so it fell gracefully over his crossed legs. He placed his arms on his lap with palms upward. He read the signs taped to the wall behind the chairs. There was a patient's bill of rights and a notice in big red print in English and Spanish demanding Medicaid, Medicare, welfare information and social security number. On the poster was scrawled a handwritten addition in English asking for private insurance carrier policy numbers.

His eyes lingered on a round symbol with a red slashed cigarette in the middle. Liz had been commanded by this symbol to leave the Buddha thought. He recalled temples in his country covered with figures of animals no one had ever seen. Designs so intricate that the mind tired as it followed the labyrinth of chiseled lines. Symbols in his country did not lead to dramatic action but forced the faithful to remain seated on a stone floor in silence.

In the front of the waiting room, five people stood leaning against the plastic divider. Three young women wore black leather jackets covered in rows of silver rivets. Their earrings made clinking sounds like tiny wind chimes when they laughed and shook their heads. They all had cropped fluorescent green hair and they snapped their fingers in time to a tune one of them was humming.

The Buddha noticed the two muscular young men next to them whose heads were shaved like a monk's. One said,

"I leveled that bastard. One punch. Pow! That's for Jamey, scumbag. Kicked his head off his fucking shoulders, Jamey did. Jamey'll make it. Whaddyathink? Our cycles beat the goddamn pigs and medics here." He landed a slow-motion, mock punch on his buddy's nose.

"Bastard slit Jamey up bad like a chicken. Jamey be OK. He's like nails."

Seated three seats to the Buddha's left was a small boy with his left arm in a thick plaster cast covered with signatures in all sizes. Names were written in red, green and orange. Daisies drawn with thin black lines wove around the cast.

The boy was emitting a low whimper like an old car left in neutral. With his free hand, he continually wiped his nose. The boy's mother or older sister, ignoring his wining and wiping read aloud in a slow voice from a comic book the boy held in his lap with his good arm.

The young woman looked up from the comic book at the Buddha. "Three whole hours he was screaming. Thank God his voice is gone. Arm itches and he can't scratch. What can I do? Doctor will help. A small emergency but another hour of that tiny whine—I'll kill him. Makes me crazy. Big emergency then, no?"

The Buddha moved over next to the boy, "Your cast is wonderful. It cures your arm. It has room for your friends to show their love." The Buddha softly stroked the cast. "Let the doctors take care when they cut away the cast. Save a piece so you can see the beautiful entwined flowers drawn on the outside and also remember the pain hidden away by the smooth inner surface."

The boy exchanged his crying for giggles, "Why are you dressed so funny? Don't you know when Halloween is? When I close my eyes I feel you tickling my arm."

"In my country, hats turned around like yours look like you are walking backwards. That would be funny. So let us laugh with each other. When I close my eyes, I also can see what is hidden. What do you hear when you close your eyes?"

"My heart goes ba-room, ba-room. That woman on the table with all those tubes—" He paused and grabbed the comic book. "Let's go home. I'm OK. Let's saw off my cast and save a couple of pieces like that guy said. Don't go crazy on me. My emergency is finito."

The woman stood up to leave, "Mister, if you were a state and federal authorized Medicaid provider, you'd make a fortune. A real fortune. Have a nice day."

The Buddha gave them a gentle nod as he saw Liz return. She slumped into the vacant seat. "That security guard is not a bad guy. I gave him a smoke. Know what he told me? Over a thousand people a day come to this ER. Three quarters with some kind of accident 'cause of drugs or booze. Half had an accident with drugs *and* booze.

"This place is the last act in fun city. If the President of the United States had something happen to him in New York, they'd bring him here. When the President is in New York, they have teams of the top surgeons waiting around. Heart surgeons, brain surgeons, chest surgeons. Secret Service sends its own doctors to check operating rooms, equipment, the works. A few dress up in white jackets and green gowns. The guard said they don't fool anyone but themselves 'cause they all have these little hearing aids stuck in one ear and bulges from their chests and belts. The security guard was pissed but now he's used to them. The Feds take away his gun so he can't become the Lone Ranger. Real control freaks."

The Buddha saw a young man writhing on a stretcher. In addition to the thick straps on the stretcher, two green-gowned orderlies held him down.

"Help me. Jesus help me," he cried. Huge elevator doors sprung open and swallowed them all up like Jonahs in the whale. The Buddha glanced up at the large wall clock.

Liz said, "We've been here half and hour and the hands on that clock haven't moved an inch. It's broken as hell. Makes you wonder how all their fancy equipment works. Bet they'll fix the clock next time the Secret Service comes. You'd think my watch was made in Switzerland. Works like a charm."

Suddenly, a voice boomed, "Get those fucking pig hands off me. Why'd you blindfold me up?" The Buddha saw a policeman pushing a young man with a thick torso, a black jacket and a shaven head into the ER. His face was wrapped like a mummy in white gauze soaked with darkened blood. As they entered the waiting room, the policeman noticed the gang members peering at him, and he pulled his revolver out of its holster. The security guard put down his newspaper, pulled out his gun and moved behind a pillar, shielding himself him from the gang.

A second cop pushed the culprit down onto an examining table. He squirmed and rolled onto his side, revealing a pair of handcuffs pinning his arms behind his back. A metal chain was connected to a pair of cuffs around his feet. He thrashed his legs out toward the cop and the handcuffs clanked against the metal rim of the examining table.

The cop held him on the table with a firm hand. "Listen fella, kick me or the doc who's coming, and I'll let you roll on the floor and dribble to death. Save the taxpayers a lot of money. Shut up. Stop screaming. There are sick people here. So your face'll have a few scars, so what? You kicked that kid's skull to pieces with those fancy boots of yours."

The cop waved his gun at the gang members, "All right all of you, sit down. Just sit down."

One of the girls shouted, "You dirty pig. You're killing my man. See what he did?" She stood up and pointed at the cop.

"Sit down and shut up. You're all going to win a free ride to the station house," the officer shouted back to them, then whispered something into his two-way radio.

"Backup's coming! Guys, split! Get on the cycles!" yelled the culprit.

The girl bellowed, "We're your family, Jamey. Fuzz can't scare us. We're staying right here."

The security guard stepped behind the pillar exposing only his head and his gun aimed at the gang.

The cop yelled at the guard, "Hey, you put your gun down. You gonna fire into the waiting room and nail a few little kids or their mothers. You're not paid minimum wage to be a goddamned hero. Just cool it."

At the back of the waiting room, four cops with drawn guns appeared. Their commander barked out an order, "OK, hands up behind your head. Walk over slow and careful and face the wall. Right now."

The five members shuffled to the wall as if it were a dance routine they knew by heart. "What did we do? Nothing. We got a right to be here. We're American citizens. We can speak. Damn fascist blue balls."

"Fine speech. Save it for the Fourth of July picnic. Frisk 'em and cuff 'em."

One of the cops patted each of the members down, "Six switchblades and three oversize nail files."

"OK, lead 'em out. Next stop, the precinct. Enjoy your stay."

Liz said to the Buddha, "Nothing to worry about. Hospitals in New York are real safe. More cops in 'em than doctors. See, two cops bring in one guy. For an emergency in the emergency room, half the cops are just an elevator ride away. Safer here than on the street at night. Hell, safer here than my block at high noon."

As the backup group of cops and their charges marched out of the waiting room, Detective Leary ran in, breathing heavily. "Got here fast as I could. Damn traffic. Siren means nothing. Great job."

When he spied Liz and the Buddha seated in back, he sauntered over to them, shaking his head in disgust. "You attract trouble or create it?"

"We're not here for a picnic. A friend—my sister's here. Broken skull. Bud's talked to a kid with a broken arm. Is that a crime or something? What's your problem?"

Ignoring her, Leary looked directly at the Buddha. "Mister, I'm going to nail you on something. Anything. If you jaywalk,

I'll bust you. Something strange. You're not normal. You think I'm stupid. That you just go around smelling the flowers?"

The Buddha replied, "Dear Detective, do not nail me for you are not a hammer. I do love flowers. In my country, some flowers are bright but lack scent. They are like fine but empty words for a man who does not mean what he speaks. Some flowers are bright and fragrant like truthful words of one who means what he speaks. Let us each say what we mean so we may become friends."

Leary reddened. He shifted his weight from side to side before replying, "In New York, we speak straight. No riddles. Just flat-out straight. You'll slip up and I'll get you." He turned on his heel like a soldier and left.

The Hospital: The Room

A young man dressed in white with a stethoscope draped around his neck approached them, "Miss, your sister will be fine. It's a bad concussion, but no excessive swelling and no damage to her brain. We've relieved the pressure. You can come back in the morning. She might not recognize you and she won't remember what happened to her, but she'll be fine. As good as new after a few days."

"Come on, Bud," Liz said, "get some rest. We'll come back in the morning before my shift."

The Buddha said, "Dear doctor, in my country, if a friend is sick, the family sits in the room until she is better. We do not bother the doctor. We just sit. If we are asked, we help."

"Well, we've got rules about visiting hours. I'm just a resident—a brand new doctor. I promise to talk to my boss. But listen, you know who's really in charge? The head nurse. If she likes you, you can sit twenty-four hours a day. She might like you. Who knows? You look real colorful and not pushy or a yeller. Come back tomorrow at seven o'clock. I'm on then. I'll take you both up. See what happens then, OK? When kids are sick, she lets mothers camp out. Who knows?"

The Buddha bowed to the doctor, "Thank you, Doctor. You are kind. You will be our guide in the morning. I will rest in this chair for the night."

"How can you rest?" whispered Liz, "These chairs are like torture. Where you gonna get food? Come on, let's go."

The Buddha replied, "Dear friend, you must rest in your home, for you have a double task of being here and working the whole day. I am used to sitting for many hours. If I am hungry, I will eat. If I am tired, I will sleep."

The calmness of the Buddha stopped Liz from arguing with him. "OK, stay. But here, take this." She thrust coins into his hand. "See that machine? Put in money and you can get a Coke or orange drink. That machine will give you a candy bar or miniature chocolate chip cookies. You won't starve. See you tomorrow."

The Buddha folded his legs under himself, rested his hands on his lap with his palms up and closed his eyes. His robe flowed down around the front of the small plastic chair so he looked as if he were seated normally with feet resting on the floor. With his eyes closed, he could envision Mary's smiling animated face as she told him about her dad becoming a real artist.

The Buddha wondered when she had last seen her father, for she spoke of him in the distant past. Perhaps in this city of eight million souls, their invisible paths might cross in the scurrying crowds at Grand Central or at the summer ice skating rink.

The Buddha felt a gentle pat on his shoulder. He opened his eyes to see the young doctor smiling down at him. Liz stood next to him. She handed the Buddha tea in a paper cup and something wrapped in a napkin. "Drink this and nosh on this bagel. It's real good. Lots of raisins. You like raisins, don't you?"

"Oh, yes. Fruit hidden in bread brings good fortune. Round bread shows the fullness of the universe. But why is the center of the bread empty?"

"I haven't a clue. Look, when we run into a rabbi, sort of like a Jewish priest, we'll get the answer."

The doctor laughed, "We have a non-denominational chapel on the seventh floor. You can continue your discussion there. Let's go up to see your sister. Here, pin these on." He handed them small plastic visitor badges.

As they walked down the hall, the doctor explained, "Your sister is down the hall in a nice room. Looks out over the East River. The other bed will probably be taken in a day or so. You can rest on it, but don't get it dirty. The nurses will kick you out if they have to redo it."

They approached the nurses' station, and the doctor said, "Hey, there's the head nurse. I'll introduce you. Miss O'Keefe, say hello to the sister and friend of the young woman in 708. Nice quiet folks. They'd like to stay in the room and won't bother anyone. They could give you all a hand if you want."

The head nurse looked up at her two visitors and continued to initial a large pile of medical files stacked up in the middle of her desk. Under her starched white cap, the Buddha saw a face covered with tiny wrinkles and two blue eyes fixed on him. "OK, doctor, if they're quiet. I'm the one responsible for visitors. I know you love this family support medicine, but I don't want my ward to turn into a hotel. Hey, you know a hotel's fine, but not a tenement. OK, go on with you."

They thanked the nurse and continued down the hall. An elderly man moved toward them with short tentative steps. He balanced himself with each step as if he were on a high wire without a net. Slightly behind him, a nurse pushed an IV drip that fed into the man's left arm. He waved his free hand at the young doctor.

"Looking good, Mr. Conrad. Another three days, you'll be walking around without that metal bottle holder. Try one more time around the block. You can do it."

The off-white walls of the corridor had cheaply framed pictures of snow-capped mountains with bubbly streams, plump, healthy young women herding sleek cows down a dirt road and apple trees obscured by white blossoms set against distant fields of wheat.

The doctor slowly pulled open the wide door to Mary's room. "She's sleeping. We'll wake her in about fifteen minutes to draw blood, take her temperature, feel her pulse, check out her eyes—the usual routine. You won't wake her if you're just talking. Just don't scream like those kids downstairs. What mouths!"

The Buddha and Liz sat down facing Mary's bed. A moveable cloth partition hid three-quarters of an empty bed and blocked their view through the large double windows.

Liz spoke in a stage whisper, "Are you still hungry, Bud? I brought you an apple and a banana, just in case. After my shift, I'll bring you more fruit and maybe some teabags we can split open. I know you love those little grains."

"Thank you, dear friend, for you are generous and thoughtful."

"Generous is no big deal. I get free meals at the restaurant. I'm not exactly skinny. The price is just too right. Thoughtful—now, that's sweet. I'll take that. Hey, look at our friend. She's opening her eyes."

Mary's eyes were wide open and staring fixedly at a spot on the ceiling. Liz jumped up suddenly and moved to the side of the bed, "Hey, hon, how ya doing? You look great."

Mary's eyes did not move, but continued to focus on the ceiling. "Think she doesn't hear us, Bud? Think she's asleep with her eyes open like that?"

"I do not know. In my country, many people can sit for hours with eyes open and see nothing that moves around them nor hear the bellow of a bull next to their ears. But in your country, in this city, in this room, I do not know."

The Buddha stared at Mary's eyes. Her dark brown pupils had expanded as if she were trapped in darkness and not the bright light of the hospital room. Two plastic lifelines snaked down to her bed. Each time a drop of fluid left from the hanging plastic bottles toward her mouth or arm, a small machine on a nightstand bleeped. Numbers flashed showing the rate and cumulative total of drops that had entered her body.

"Jesus," Liz exclaimed, "I feel sad, like she's really my sister. Gotta get back to the grind. See you tonight, Bud."

The Buddha closed his eyes and placed his hands palms-up on his lap.

As morning light filtered into the room, Mary opened her eyes. "Where am I? Who's there? Bud? Where am I? Oh yeah, ice skating like a little kid. That's it, snatched up a kid like a circus acrobat."

The young doctor entered the room. "If you'll just leave for a few minutes, sir, while I examine the patient..."

The Buddha stood in the hallway, observing orderlies as they pushed hospital beds down the halls, waving and smiling at one another.

When the doctor came back out he reported, "She's recovering nicely. She'll be out in no time. Please, go back in."

Mary had her head propped up on a pillow and spoke to the Buddha, "The doc wants me to take these little green pills for the next week. Three a day—morning, noon and night. You have a lot of drugstores in your country?"

"No, but in every town and village, we have men who give herbs, crushed earth or flower petals to neighbors in need."

"Sounds delicious. Does it work?"

"Oh, certainly, my dear friend. It brings back health if those who give and those who take are believing."

"Sure, old, sick cynics don't fade away, they just die. Your country must be placebo heaven."

"If you do not believe that health returns aided by our homemade medicines, or you have an evil mind when seeking them, no patient gets better." He continued, "In a small village, I met a man of medicine who was known throughout his valley for his wonderful cures. One day, a stranger approached him as he sat in his yard with his bottles, bundles and baskets full of medicines.

"The stranger said, 'In my village on the other side of the river, many are sick. They stay in bed all day. They barely eat. Some speak not at all. Their spirits are gone.'

"The man of medicine replied, 'I have mixed an elixir which lifts the spirit. But listen carefully, for one drop must be placed into a large bottle of water like this, which I will also give you. With a single drop in the bottle, the spirit returns and they will start to talk and smile. However, if a drop goes into a small glass of water, the elixir will destroy the spirit. The afflicted will crave the elixir at all times, trade all their possessions for another drink and kill to drink more. Gentle stranger, my elixir will not work unless you sample it first yourself after you have mixed it. Take a small sip and wait twenty-four hours before you give it to the sick. Follow these instructions or my elixir is useless.'

"The stranger said, 'I will mix it as you instruct, taste it myself, wait twenty-four hours and give it freely to my neighbors.' He emptied all the gold coins from his pockets onto the ground and left with the large bottle and the elixir.

"The man of medicine told me that he had sensed the stranger was evil and feared he would drug his neighbors, take all their goods and change them into people who rob and kill. So, he had given him an elixir that cured if diluted in the large bottle, but would cause vomiting and hair to fall out if given in strong doses. The stranger would not be hurt. Hair grows back and vomiting stops. He would learn that following honest advice heals, but following evil greed leads to harm.

"How did the man of medicine know the stranger was evil?" I asked. He replied, 'An honest man would have saved some coins for his family or to give to the poor on the way back to his village. An evil man gives all his coins believing that his wealth will multiply when he creates his deadly drug.'"

The Hospital Room: Why Live?

A nurse knocked softly on the door and then entered with a man and a woman. She stopped in front of the vacant bed and explained to them, "Great view of the river. Now you just change into this gown, Mr. Bello. Your wife will take your clothes home. After the operation tomorrow, you'll be home in a week. Better than ever. I'll be back in ten minutes."

She shook her head in disbelief as she passed the Buddha on her way out. "This city's becoming a circus. Guys in robes with their eyes closed," she muttered to herself.

The Buddha heard an irregular bleeping sound that drowned out Mary's shallow breathing. Loud sobs came from behind the screen followed by a continual low moan and deep breaths that caused the cloth screen to undulate like a sail. A violent metallic screech gave way to a strong breeze that cooled the Buddha's face.

With a start, he opened his eyes. The huge old-fashioned hospital window was pulled up. A man dressed in a green hospital gown was seated on the ledge with his feet dangling down on the side of the building. The man clutched the side of the window frame with one arm and edged himself even farther out on the narrow ledge. The Buddha heard more of the same low moans.

The man shifted his gaze from the street far below and half glancing at the Buddha, cried out in a staccato voice, "I'm going to die!" With his free hand, he crossed himself. "Why live?" he said, as he moved out a little farther on the ledge.

The Buddha moved his arms so they rested interlocked in his lap.

"Don't move. One step at me, I jump."

The door to the hospital room swung open silently behind the Buddha causing the wind from the window to whip through the room. The head nurse entered with an older doctor who was built like a marine with white hair in a crew cut.

The Buddha remained motionless as the breeze fluttered up the bottom of his robe. He responded to the man in the window, "Dear friend, I can remain still for hours. I shall not move. You say, 'Why live?' That question fascinates many but interests me not. Is the question not *why live*, but instead, *how to live*?"

"Shut up! You confuse me. I'm confused enough. I want to jump."

"Jump if you desire, but understand that to do so would instead answer the question, 'How to die?'"

"Mister, maybe your question is not so stupid. Let me think." He turned to face the Buddha and swung his legs around so they rested on the floor. The man saw the nurse and doctor who had entered the room. The doctor's face was calm, yet the man could see the anger in his eyes. The doctor whispered to the nurse who left the room and closed the door softly behind her.

The doctor took three swift steps into the middle of the room so he stood between the patient and the Buddha. His voice was very controlled as he spoke. "Why, Mr. Bello, how are you today? Now just come away from that window. We don't want that dirty city air coming into our clean hospital now, do we?"

Bello looked at the doctor as if he were crazy. "How am I? How am I? How would you be if you were going to be cut open tomorrow and you read in your chart that the CAT scan found metastases in your spinal cord and brain? Stop! You're gonna make me jump right now."

"You read your chart well, but that's the purpose of the operation. We'll cut out the tumor and those few cells that have spread. You'll be home in no time. You'll be fine. You have my word as a physician. Let's shake on it." He took three more steps toward Bello and stuck out his right hand like a harpoon.

Bello started to extend his arm but stopped. "Ask him. Ask the guy behind you what he thinks."

"Looking at him, I don't think he speaks English. Do you understand English?" The doctor spoke without taking his eyes off of Bello.

"I know he speaks English. I just spoke to him. Ask him."

The doctor's face was frozen into a grim, smiling mask. "Well, it doesn't matter if he speaks or not. I am your doctor and I'm here to help you. Just shake hands." He took another step toward Bello who was burrowing into the corner like a child trying to hide.

Suddenly, the doctor lunged forward and grabbed him around the wrist. Bello pivoted toward the window, screaming as his arm twisted in the doctor's grip. His legs were out the window and with his free arm, he was pushing himself farther out on the ledge.

The doctor yelled, "Nurse! Nurse, come on! Come on!" He now held onto Bello with two hands.

The Buddha stood up and the doctor yelled at him, "Sit down, fella. I can handle this. Don't interfere."

With a desperate push, the patient fell from the ledge. The doctor lunged forward like a fisherman who had just hooked a whale, screaming in pain as Bello's weight bent his fingers backwards. The nurse and two burly orderlies rushed past the Buddha, knocking him back toward his seat. As one orderly reached down for him, Bello pushed off from the wall like a backstroker at the start of a long race. There was a long silence followed by a thud as Bello hit the concrete parking lot twenty-two stories down.

The doctor stared down at the fish that got away. "My God, what did I...Nurse, move the other patient to another room on the ward. Take her friend out too. This room will become bedlam. Right now."

The orderlies rolled in a platform and gently moved Mary onto it. The nurse unplugged the electronic monitors and pushed the IV drips as they wheeled Mary out of the room.

The Buddha turned to the doctor. "You chose to save him by an operation. You also chose to save him from jumping, but he chose to die. Do not blame yourself when a man makes his own choice."

"Thanks! It's crap like that that made him jump. Now get out."

When the nurse returned, the doctor said, "The patient was crazy or maybe depressed. Let's minimize the circus. That guy in the robe didn't see a thing seated behind the curtain. He barely speaks English and he talks funny. Now, we don't want the press to interview someone like that, do we? It's bad enough to have a headline screaming, 'Patient jumps rather than face operation at Memorial.' It sorta undoes all those mushy feel-good TV ads about how we care for each patient."

"Yes, doctor. They're moved to the other ward. No one will bother them."

In Mary's new, identical room, she was placed in the bed next to the window. Her eyes remained closed. "All rooms are the same to her," the Buddha mused.

From the chair, he could see a river half-hidden in black. Far in the distance, a huge sign framed a one-word message: "PEPSI." The Buddha wondered if this was a warning message to all the people on this side of the river. In his country, hospitals were simple structures. There were no elevators or complicated machines. "Hospitals in my country lack much," thought the Buddha, "but they also lack guns, policemen, doctors with gruff hearts and patients that jump out of windows." He placed his hands on his lap palms-up and closed his eyes.

Just then, Liz walked into the room. "Good evening, Bud. I brought some goodies for dinner. Try these," she said, as she unveiled two bananas, a handful of small tangerines and one large navel orange. "Just peel and eat. Sanitary. Untouched by dirty human hands. No fork or knife necessary. Enjoy." She spread out the classified section of her newspaper on the Buddha's lap like a black and white tablecloth.

"Thank you, my dear friend."

They heard a soft knock on the door.

"Come in," boomed Liz.

The young doctor who had escorted them up the day before entered. "Time to take her temperature and get the pulse. Twice a day—six in the morning and six at night."

"Hope you can wake her up, Doc. If she were really sleeping normal, why would you wake her at six in the morning?" Liz asked.

"Miss, now don't quote me, but this is a hospital. Shifts change at six and six. A new shift always starts with a temperature check. Hospitals are run for the convenience of the staff, not the patient. Get it?"

"Even in a famous hospital like this," replied Liz. "You like this headline? Maybe you'll autograph my copy." She held up the front page of the tabloid with the enormous headline, "WAS JUMPING BETTER THAN AN OPERATION?"

The doctor focused on Mary's pulse. "Her pulse is holding steady. I'd bet that by tomorrow, she'll be able to speak and see. Hey, you know anything about that suicide? Were you switched to this room before or after that tragedy?"

"This happened in her room?" Liz exclaimed. "Let's hear it, Bud!"

The Buddha replied, "What I saw will not restore life. What I say will not restore truth neglected by your newspaper. Listen with an open heart to your patients, my young healer, so you can give hope for life and trust for truth to flourish."

The doctor replied, "Sounds good. I rotate out of this ward tonight. I'll come back in three days to say goodbye when you check out. I like to follow my patients, but they seem to disappear from me."

"OK, Doc," Liz said. "If we miss you, I promise my sister will come back to thank you. When she can see, she'll see you're cute."

The Home at the End of the Tunnel: The Mole People

Mary blinked in the strong morning sun as they hailed a cab at the main exit of Bellevue. "Well, a week in the hospital, and good as new. Nice of my doc to call. I'll come back sometime to say hello."

The young doctor had said goodbye to the Buddha over the house phone as he was dealing with a ruptured appendix. He implored the Buddha to make sure Mary kept eating.

"Remember the first drips of sugar water from that long tube into my arm? Then every day, special thick chocolate milkshakes served with every meal. Delicious."

The Buddha smiled at Mary. She did look better.

"Have you ever devoured so much ice cream?" the Buddha asked.

"Not in the Big Apple. Here they whip the ice cream, make it light and fluffy. Looks big, but they sell air. We made ice cream at home. I'd get to turn the crank till my arms gave up. Dad would flex his muscles and let me touch his arm. Then he'd turn the crank so fast it hummed. Favorite flavor was fresh peach from our tree. Dad would let us eat till we'd explode. Mom said I was disgusting acting like a pig.

You know, sometimes she'd made a truly revolting dish like macaroni with melted cheese. If I didn't eat it all, she'd say, 'Think of all the starving children in China, dear.' Never could win with her."

The Buddha said, "Every act in the world is woven like an infinite spider web with every other act. The flapping of a butterfly's wings in the village can be felt in the palace of the king, days away by foot."

"You think my mother was right? If I leave overcooked macaroni, do children starve?"

The Buddha reflected to himself, "At my next meditation, I will clear my mind of all images except that of a small American girl leaving macaroni on her plate and children starving. The thread binding them may make itself visible."

Mary and the Buddha entered a cab.

"Riverside Park and Seventy-second," Mary chimed out.

"What number, Miss?"

"No number. Just in the park by the basketball court in back."

As the Buddha left the cab, he saw the Hudson River with the rocky cliffs of New Jersey on the far side.

"Come on, Bud," Mary yelled as she walked toward a high wire fence. The Buddha turned around and saw a large sign that said in bold black letters, "KEEP OUT—HIGH VOLTAGE WIRES."

A red skull and crossbones had been spray-painted on the sign, along with huge yellow letters proclaiming: "SAL WAS HERE."

Mary had stopped in front of a sheet of plywood on the ground by the fence. As the Buddha approached, she moved the plywood to one side, revealing a three-foot-wide hole dug under the fence. "Come on, Bud, scoot under here."

"Is this not dangerous with hurtling trains and bolts of electricity?" asked the Buddha.

"Bud, you want to know danger? Stay on that side of the

fence in the park at night. Come on, meet my friends. Home sweet home. Safe and sound. Free coffee. Maybe tea."

The Buddha gingerly put his feet into the hole and ducked under the fence. Mary grabbed a makeshift handle fastened to the underside of the plywood and pulled it back to cover the secret entrance.

She took the Buddha's hand and pulled him toward a tunnel with a series of train tracks running down the middle. "Ever lived in a tunnel?" she asked.

"We do not have tunnels made by man in my country. But I have spent months with religious hermits in caves made by water dripping out from the mountain."

"Same thing. My friends are hermits too. Not religious. People call 'em homeless, but this is their home. I lived here off and on. Specially when I was broke."

"My dear friend, you are not broke. Those kind doctors fixed your head. They say it is strong."

Mary tugged the Buddha through the tunnel in complete darkness. About a hundred feet ahead, he noticed light pouring down through a grate casting a striped pattern on the tunnel floor. As they continued deeper into the tunnel, the Buddha saw the amber glow of fire. Laughter echoed from the concrete walls. If he had not seen two men sitting next to the fire, he would have thought there was a large crowd gathered.

"Hey, Can Man. Hey, Scoop. It's me." Mary waved excitedly at the two men by the fire. "Need some coffee. Tea for my friend."

Can Man stood up and peered into the darkness. His hair was long and matted, his beard was white and scruffy and reached down to his chest.

When Mary and the Buddha walked under the spotlight from the overhead grate, he yelled out, "Mary's come home for a visit. Hey, Scoop, Miss Lazarus has just returned from the living."

Scoop bent in front of the fire and grabbed a pot from a grill resting on two cinderblocks. He poured the rich brown coffee into an old glass beer mug. "Welcome to our humble home. Here's mud in your eye."

He handed Mary a glass, stared at the Buddha and said, "We've entertained cops in blue, nurses in white, Amtrak guys in brown. But never a guy in a bright yellow robe. Welcome, friend. Water for tea pronto."

The Buddha sat down on a thin pile of old newspapers congealed into a cushion. He sat down cross-legged. He had sat like this for hours, under trees, in mud huts or in caves with the hermits. If left alone, he meditated. If people were present, he could still meditate or just sit, talk or listen.

Scoop had his brown hair close-cropped like a soldier. A huge pair of goggles was pushed up on his head and he wore a one-piece black Lycra shirt and shorts, with the word, "Scoop" written in scroll-like script on the chest. Around his neck he wore a thick shiny metal chain fastened with a huge padlock.

Scoop handed the Buddha tea in a tall glass and said, "You arrived just in time. Five minutes, I gotta leave for work. What a drag, but I'm the best bike messenger in all of New York. I scoop up the package and deliver it fast like a speeding bullet. It's a race. Always get tips. Biggest Wall Street offices ask for me to deliver. See the old Scoopmobile over there?"

The Buddha saw a bike, black and polished to a high gloss in the dim light. "Yes, dear friend. I thank you for the tea. I have never seen so beautiful a bicycle. In my village, the bicycles are coated with mud. With only one or two in a village, there are no races. The paths and single road have brown puddles that swallow up unsuspecting riders. Even a rider bearing a message for the king must travel mindfully or risk his tire being chewed by a sharp rock hidden like a crocodile at the bottom of the puddle."

"Hey Bud," Mary laughed, "your village is like New York. I've seen guys from two truck outfits go around at night to make the potholes even deeper. Good for business. You know what I mean?"

Scoop chimed in, "If Con Ed's construction sign is stolen, you drop twelve feet into a maze of wires and get fried. Your guys are lucky you only have crocodile rocks to deal with. You like our home? High ceilings, very private. Quiet except for the damn trains. Good neighbors. We share whatever we got."

The Buddha stared at the shaft of light filtering down the granite block wall. A slow trickle of water wended its way toward the floor. Three mattresses were neatly arranged in a line on wooden shipping pallets. Each mattress had a sleeping bag on it. The fluffy sleeping bags were all a bright orange and practically shone in the eternal twilight. Huge plastic buckets full of water rested on rickety folding chairs.

"You like the looks of our home?" Scoop asked again.

"What you see is what you see," the Buddha said as he nodded his head toward Scoop.

Scoop leaned over to Can Man and said in a low voice, "This guy is weird. Yellow robe, sandals—I don't see no beach. Talks English funny. If Mary digs him, he's OK by me."

"Your small wall is wonderful," the Buddha said.

"So, you like the arrangement of those plastic milk cartons?" Can Man gestured to the red cartons that formed a large irregular outline around the makeshift furniture.

"Oh yes, dear friend. Your wall is quite special. It does not support a roof so it can be weak. It lets everyone see through it so there is nothing to hide. Its strong color is like a sun in your world which the sun rarely visits."

"Oh yeah, I get it," Can Man said. "Everything here we built or bought. Nothing stolen. We're not crooks. We all chipped in: Scoop's tips, money from can returns and panhandling. Maybe the deli wasn't throwing out those beautiful cartons, but they looked thrown out to us."

The Buddha smiled and then asked, "Can returns and handling pans? What does this mean, friend?"

Like a tenured professor before a special ed class, Can Man stood up, "Really simple. City Hall wants to collect a few more pennies so folks have to pay a little extra to get the cans but they're too lazy or too busy to return 'em and get their pennies back. So most people just throw the cans away. I pick the cans off the street, turn 'em in and get money. Nickels from heaven. They add up. Everyone is happy. People let me make an honest dollar, the city is cleaner and cans live again. Maybe a lowly Sprite becomes a Miller High Life. You get it? The cans are re-in-CAN-ated. Panhandling just means begging. You hold the pan out by its handle and let money drop in."

"Oh yes, in my country, all the sages beg. I have begged for many years. I beg for food and for coins. I beg from rich. Also, I beg from the poor. It is considered better to beg from the poor for they do not have as many chances to show the goodness of a generous nature. When I finish I sit under a tree and share with other travelers or go to a cave of a wise hermit."

Can Man sprinkled water on the fire. "No more fire till dinner. We all got work to do." The fire hissed and emitted a white steamy cloud.

"Mister, you ever run into the Pope?" asked Can Man. "I saw the Pope riding down Broadway in the Popemobile. He stood up in the back under this plastic bubble. Bulletproof, I bet. He was waving his left hand and then his right. Tiring, I guess. Who'd wanna kill the Pope? Nuts everywhere. Ever been shot at, Mister?"

The Buddha replied, "Though I have never met any Pope, they are wise and gentle men. They give a message to their flock from the word of their God. But the Word that can be talked about is not the true Word. The name that can be named is not the eternal Name."

Can Man asked, "Shot at?"

"Oh yes. Once in the forest, an arrow pierced my arm. A hunter who had been chasing a wild boar crashed through the bamboo forest and came upon me. He cried, 'Forgive me, dear Master, forgive me. Do not hate me.'

"'Why should I hate you?,' I replied. 'I do not hate the rich who give me no alms. I do not hate the sages who tell the people that they must fast their bodies into skeleton shapes if they are to know the word. My arm will recover. I am not attached to it the way it is attached to me. The decay of my body I do not fear. The body is a sacred vessel that cannot be owned. If you try to possess it, you will destroy it. If you try to hold onto it, you will lose it.'"

Can Man picked up a huge neatly folded fishing net. "See, I put the cans in the net and let the stuff drain out. It's not so heavy. I'm a city fisherman. Environmentally correct. Not an endangered can ever caught in my net. Ever fish, Mister?"

"No, I do not fish, but the people in my village fish. They weave their nets from the palm and make them long as a man. Then they secure them in the stream with rocks and sticks. As the fish swim down toward the sea, a few catch themselves by going into the net. The villagers believe that they do not harm the fish, since the fish chooses to be caught. But I say that words strung together like hooks can curve in or out and make day night. The words hurt and the words hide the deadly barbs. So I do not eat the fish, though the villagers must for the strength to work in the fields while I sit cross-legged taking or gathering alms."

Scoop had wiped his bike clean with a rag and squirted oil in the gearshift. "Mary, you know that social worker? The smiling, cheery black woman who wants us to move out? Give us each a room? What you think?"

"Yes, yes, yes. Own private space. Electricity. Turn on the lights instead of this twenty-four hour darkness. Listen to the Dead on a CD player. You're not a mole. Oh, yes."

"Yeah, private is nice when you want to pee. Specially for you, Mary. Let's just suppose I have my own room. So I put a lock on it 'cause I got neighbors I don't know. I gotta hide my money. Maybe in a book I could hollow out 'cause if people come in you don't want a cigar box or something that says 'steal me.' Then maybe I get a second lock to protect my money." Scoop put his black helmet on. "With a CD or TV, I have to get a fox lock."

The Buddha had a perplexed look on his face.

"It's not about animals, Mister, It's a long metal pole that you stick in the floor and angle it up against the door so you can't bust it open. So locked away in my room, who would know me? If I were sick, who'd care for me? Not smiling Aunt Jemima. She be on the next case. Mary, you need a rest. We make you food. We all tell stories by the fire like fancy kids at camp. You bring old Yellow Robe. He can stay too. Still you're right, it's still no fun to pee. What do you think, Mister?"

The Buddha smiled, as he liked to pee in the light so he could create his own momentary waterfall.

"In my country, there are huge deep caves where the monks live. Along the winding corridors, there are little rooms or cells hollowed from the rock. Each monk has his room. There are no doors. The monks do not chat in the cave. There are no hellos, goodbyes, have a nice days. If a monk is sick or feels lonely, the other monks are with him. They bring him special tea with curing herbs. They sit and tell stories of what they have seen outside the cave that day. The monks all gather outside the cave in the morning and sit quietly for two hours deep in meditation. They are together, but each is separate. When the gong sounds, they arise and follow the paths to the fields and villages to beg for alms. In the evening, all the money collected is put in a large pot and all the food is cooked at the big central fire, so they may all share the gifts they have received."

Can Man covered his ears as a train thundered by and shook the plastic milk carton walls. "Living here, we might as well be blind and those trains make you deaf faster than going to your Dead concerts, Mary. Hey, see that big flashlight bopping this way? Bet it's Aunt Jemima bringing us pancakes."

A heavyset black woman waving an enormous flashlight like a wand approached the group. She was neatly dressed in a light beige suit. "Hey folks, I got good news and bad news."

Can Man's booming voice echoed off the walls of the tunnel. "New York City social work babble talk makes good sound like bad and bad like good. Tell us what you got and we can have a contest to guess what's bad and what's good. First prize a ride on Scoop's bike. Second prize be two rides. Even you can enter, Ms. Jemima, but don't break de bank or break de bike if you win."

"Oh, Can Man," the social worker replied, "you should be on *Saturday Night Live* with that sharp tongue. Never mind, here's the news. In half an hour, the city will send cops to drag you out of here and build cinderblock walls so you can't get back in. Now the City also got you each a private room in an SRO hotel. The government will pay all your rent. So there it is. I worked hard to get this and I'll help you in your new place."

Can Man slumped forward. He wiped his eyes, pretending to brush out a speck of dust. He said in a soft voice, "I know you wanna help us. But we're not homeless. We got a family here. We care for each other. Look, Mary just got out of the hospital, she can stay here. We'll bring her food. Even her friend, Mister Yellow Robe is welcome to stay. Our family gets larger and smaller like kids who leave for college and come back with their buddies. It's the end for me. Seal me in here like an Egyptian king. In three thousand years, break the wall down and let an archeologist find a New York mummy. I'm doomed. Don't save me, just seal me in."

Scoop said, "Seal me in, too. Bury me with my bike. It's all I have, just like the Egyptians kings. Maybe I have Egyptian blood in me."

Mary sat down on a plastic carton and hid her face in her hands. She began to sob.

The social worker's face turned to an ebony mask of sadness. Then in a steady voice she said, "We don't bury folks alive in New York. Even if you all want it. No way. If the cops drag you out, they'll take you to a shelter. Not the rooms I arranged."

Can Man and Scoop stood like silent boulders. Mary continued to sob.

The social worker continued, "This is a great deal for all of you. I fought my supervisor who said, 'Throw the moles in a shelter. Save your energy for where you can do some good. The moles can't make it out in the light.' I can't fight everyone for you folks by myself. Goodbye and good luck."

Figure the Odds

"Fifteen minutes till the cops come," Scoop yelled. "I'll be ready. Took on tougher dudes than New York cops in Vietnam. I'll mow 'em down like pop-up targets in a country fair shooting gallery." He stepped forward into the glare of the flashlight. His left arm was cocked carrying something hidden under a dirty white towel.

A trickle of water ran down the middle of the tunnel. The walls were perspiring like a runner on a hot summer day. The muddy water curled around the campsite turning it into a temporary island.

The social worker aimed her flashlight at Can Man. "Is Scoop nuts? Even if there's nothing but his hairy arm under that towel—threaten cops? They'll shoot first and maybe ask questions later. Can Man, talk sense to him. Vietnam! What he want? A military funeral?" She glanced at her watch and waved it at Scoop. "Look at this, Mister General, cops due in ten minutes. This poor sick girl, that guy in the robes. Want them sprayed with lead? You told me you're a gambler, but this is suicide. Odds are ten thousand to nothing you'll be history."

Mary continued to cry as she lay on the mattress. She reached a hand out toward the Buddha and he pulled her up. "Let's split, Bud. Came here to rest, not my final resting place. Less than ten minutes. Don't want to bump into cops at the main entrance to this five star hotel." Mary saw a deck of playing cards held together by a twisted rubber band next to Scoop. "So, Scoop, you a big-time gambler?"

"Yeah. Worked my way through Yale by majoring in poker. In Nam, only played with officers. No grunts. Still got money in the old bank."

Can Man spoke up, "Hey folks, seven minutes the fuzz arrives. Let's chat outside."

Scoop shook his head from side to side. His arm rested on two plastic cartons piled on top of each other. The towel remained around his arm.

Mary glared at Scoop. "Here's the deal, big shot," she said reaching down the front of her dress, pulling out a ten-dollar bill and waving it in Scoop's face." Put the deck of cards in your hand. Good, now take off the rubber band. Well done. If my buddy, Mister Yellow Robe, can guess the third card from the top—and you deal 'em—you give me what you have wrapped under the towel plus a ten spot and we all leave pronto. Real pronto. If he doesn't guess right, I give you the tenner and we all wait right here for the big shoot-out. Figure the odds, Scoop. One out of fifty-two or however many cards in that ratty deck."

Scoop laughed, "Sure, Mary. It's a sucker bet, Mister. You better believe in miracles. Ready? Here goes…"

At the entrance to the tunnel, voices echoed toward them. "Anyone here? Police!" The voices continued, "Keep coming guys. Shine the light here."

The Buddha nodded to Scoop, "I do not believe in miracles. I do not gamble. But I can see my way clear. So, as you say, we can all clear out of here." The Buddha lifted his robes slightly to avoid the mud-thickened water that had risen a few inches, decreasing the size of their island.

As the Buddha smiled, he recalled his trip to the great forest pool where the lotus plant grows with roots deep in the rich mud. "All the plants have their roots in the mud. Some plants strive upward, but their heads remain submerged and never reach the surface. Some plants barely reach the surface and float upon it. Yet still other plants thrust their heads out of the water and flower in full splendor. It seems that many stand ready to understand the teachings. Some would hear it but not grasp it. Others would neither hear nor understand. Yet, all strive upwards, seeking the light because just like the lotus, it is their nature to do so."

Mary leaned over to the Buddha whispering, "Close your eyes so you can see. Can you see the third card?"

With his eyes now closed, the Buddha responded, "It is a five, for we are five. A red card, not hard like a diamond, but brave like a heart."

Scoop flipped off the top card with his free hand. "Jack of clubs." Quickly he let the second card fall. "Eight of spades." He paused with a slight sideways shake of his arm covered by the towel. He held the third card facedown in front of Mary. "This is it. Here she comes." He turned over the third card with a slow-motion gesture. "Son of a bitch. Five of hearts! How'd you do that, Mister? Cards never left my hands."

"I'm gonna pull off that dirty towel," said Mary. "Give me your tenspot. Explanations are extra." She gave the towel a swift yank. Laughter erupted as they all stared at the small black fold-up umbrella clutched in his hand. "OK, Scoop, take your bike. Can Man, bring those cans. I'll take the dishes. Let's follow this muddy brick road to our new home. Scoop, old buddy, why don't you open up your umbrella. Probably raining outside. You know the odds, don't you?"

Your Pockets Are There to Remind Me

Two strong flashlights focused on the group as they made their way out. A disembodied voice yelled, "OK, folks, got all your stuff together? Come this way. Hurry, tide is rising."

"We're coming, Officers." The social worker replied in a cheery voice. She turned behind her, "Come on there. City can't pay enough to make me walk through all this mud. Mole folks coming out 'cause of some card trick. Beats guns, I guess."

"Come on Auntie. Why don't you part the water like Moses?" Scoop laughed.

"Walk on it like Jesus?" added Can Man.

"Well, well," the social worker exclaimed, "didn't think you all were so religiously inclined. In your new house, a bible's put in every bedroom."

The group straggled single-file toward the policemen. The social worker led the parade with Mary at the end, carrying a large red plastic carton filled with folded clothes.

As he saw the group slowly ambling toward him, one of the cops barked, "Let's get the show moving. The bricklayers are right behind us. Don't want to be sealed in like some dead pharaoh with his live family. I've seen enough mummies in the museum."

The procession made its way slowly past him. He waved his arms. "Come on, come on." His arm brushed against Mary who began to slip in the mud. He plucked at her and held her upright.

"First time I've been saved by a cop. Thanks."

The officer blushed slightly at the ironic compliment. "Sorry, didn't mean to give you a mud bath." He smiled a large toothy grin.

The second cop, a tall and skinny man by the name of Mallory approached his young trim partner. "Cone, my boots are muddy and I just shined them. It's a wonderful place here. The smell of sewers, trains sound like they're barreling right at you, and my rookie partner thinks he's an archeologist. Next tour, let's hang out in Grant's tomb. You know who's buried in Grant's tomb?"

"Yeah, I know," laughed Mary. "Karl Marx's brother, Groucho." The entire group including the two cops started to laugh. The Buddha was puzzled. He thought, if the answer is in the question, why do you need the answer?

The Little Fish Come Out Blind

As the group stumbled from the tunnel, Mary heard the loud drone of cars whishing down the West Side Highway. She blinked in the strong morning sun as she gazed out at the Hudson's gentle slate gray waves.

Both policemen put on their one-way mirror aviation glasses. Scoop took out a carefully folded white rag and started to wipe mud from his bike. "Give me the address of the new digs. I'll be there by six. Have dinner on the table, Mary. Gotta go, business is calling." He tossed the rag to the cops and said, "Here you go. Shine 'em up, Officer."

"Wait a minute, Scoop," the social worker began, "the apartment's so nice. Don't you want to see your room? When you last live in a room? Know how hard it is to find an apartment in this city? Landlords don't line up to rent to homeless. But mole people? Forget it. Broke the rules a little for you. Told a—pardon the expression—little white lie. Said you all lived in a very quiet place the city was tearing down. Said you worked on Wall Street and Can Man was in an environmental business. Didn't mention no Mary or a guy dressed up in a robe."

Cone said, "You got a signed lease? He took the rent deposit I bet. No sweat then. We'll help you move in, but no tips please." He walked over to Mary. "I'll carry that carton for you. You OK? You look real pale."

"Gee thanks, Officer. Of course I'm pale. Not much light in the rooms at Bellevue. Stay in a cave long enough, you get real pale and turn blind. Ever see fish that lived in caves for centuries? The little fish come out blind. Honest."

Mallory whispered, "She's cute, but a fruitcake from Bellevue. You definitely don't need that, Cone."

Cone looked at the carton. There were folded blouses and jeans sticking out from a Super Rite plastic bag, three books all identically covered by red and white Hunter college book covers. A bulging purse made out of alligator green plastic took up half the space in the carton.

"Must have been tough to read in that cave, Miss."

"Call me Mary. Say hello to my friend, Bud." She paused as Cone glanced warningly at the Buddha. She added in a low voice, "He's not my boyfriend. You know what I mean. He's just a friend, you know."

"Oh sure." Cone's cheeks turned slightly red. His brown curly hair stuck out from his cap like a suppressed Afro. "So what were you reading down there?"

"Can't read down there. I got a notebook so I could write in that muck. Hope I can read my chicken scrawls. These books, I read 'em and reread 'em. *Great Gatsby*, *Billy Budd*, *The Trial*. Used to study English Lit. Ever read them?"

"Not *Gatsby* or *Billy Budd*, but Kafka's my favorite. *The Castle*, *Amerika*, "The Metamorphosis." That *Trial* was really scary. Being guilty without even knowing what crime you were supposed to have committed! Policemen in New York have to go to college now to get somewhere."

The group crossed the park toward the jumble of apartment buildings that comprised Riverside Drive. Two young mothers were chatting on a park bench. One yelled to the children playing in an earth-colored sandbox. "Kids, look over there. A tiny parade with police but no music."

Mallory and the social worker led the parade. The cop's boots were shiny but the social worker's low-heeled shoes were still caked with mud. Can Man trailed them by ten feet, lugging a plastic carton and a huge net clanking with soft drink cans and bottles that he had picked up in the park. The Buddha walked alone followed by the two stragglers. Officer Cone carried Mary's red carton, and Mary walked beside him, swinging her arms back and forth like an athlete limbering up for a race.

A young girl climbed out of the sandbox and, pail in hand, ran to the social worker. "Wanna buy our delicious homemade mud pie? Just one nickel."

"No, young lady," the social worker said. "Does your mother let you eat mud pies?"

"She tell me not to eat my mud pies but it's OK to make pies. Never sold one. Not till now. Mud pies. Mud pie mix. Tastes great."

Officer Cone came forward. Reaching into his pocket, he pulled out a nickel. "Don't want it right now, 'cause it'll spoil my lunch, but I'll take one delicious-looking mud pie to go. Got something for me to carry it in?" The child shook her head slowly. She gazed at the nickel in Cone's hand, which seemed to be growing smaller by the second.

"That's OK." Cone said. "Take the nickel anyway." She pocketed the coin and gave Cone a big grin.

Druggie Supermarket

Cone continued on alongside Mary. "So how long have you lived in the city, Miss?"

"Not too long. Beats the flatlands."

"Do you have any family here?"

Mary stared at her feet. "Well, I am looking for my father. I think he's somewhere in the city. Could take a long time to find him—this is not some little village."

"Is your mother here too, or is she back home?"

"My mother is dead. Hit by a car. Alcohol did it."

"I'm sorry. These drunken drivers. They should all be locked up."

"No, the driver wasn't drunk. It was my mother. Used to yell at my dad. Said he didn't love her, never earned enough. Said he pretended to be a big-shot artist. She began to drink and pretended she didn't. Hid bottles at the bottom of the garbage cans. Stuck them behind the cereal boxes or under the sofa. Finally, my dad said if she didn't stop, he'd move out and take me with him. He went through the house searching for bottles. Threw them out one by one into a metal garbage can. She heard the glass breaking and smelled the alcohol.

Screamed like a crazy person. Swore on the Holy Mother she'd never take another drop."

"So what happened? Turn out OK?"

"Kept cold sober for two months, then she got into a fight with my uncle, slammed the door, marched to the nearest bar, got so drunk she could barely walk, and stumbled in front of a car on her way home. God have mercy on her soul. Nice woman. Took me to see Bambi and Snow White as many times as I wanted when I was a kid. No miracles in my town."

It Gives Life or Death

The patrol car pulled up in front of an apartment building. It hinted of long past glories hidden behind the prison-like bars over every first-story window. Two concrete lions with missing tails and broken ears marked the entrance, the brick pedestals on which they stood were covered by psychedelic graffiti. A rusted metal framework designed to support a canvas canopy extended to the curb. One forlorn strip of canvas remained fluttering in the wind with faded black numerals: 3-6-0-0.

Mallory said in a jovial voice, "Let's wait for the doorman to take up the new tenants' matching luggage. Red plastic is in this year."

Cone replied, "My grandparents lived around here when they came from Germany in the thirties. The doorman spoke only Yiddish. I bet he died fifty years ago."

"Listen, Mallory," Cone began again. "I'm gonna talk to her about what I found. Confront her like you said." He patted the syringe tucked in his front pocket. Cops are supposed to help people. Community outreach."

"There's only one thing you want to reach out and touch. Stay away. You think she supported her habit by teaching English literature?"

The social worker's car pulled up behind the policemen. She waved and gave them three rapid beeps from her horn.

Mallory laughed, "Oughta bust her. Look at that sign." He nodded toward the sign that said, "No Honking—$100 Fine."

"No way. I don't need to look for more trouble," replied Cone.

A slim man with a backwards baseball cap and a blue knit tie bounded through the door toward the social worker. "I started to worry. You never get here. Why the cops?"

"Oh, they're just extra helpful. No problems," she said. "It's those three in the car plus another guy be here by six, after work. Need five keys." The man looked puzzled. She continued, "Fifth key for me. I pay the rent, don't I?" She gave a beckoning wave at her car, "Everybody out, folks. Your new home."

The Buddha stared at the bars on the windows. "In my country," he thought, "jail windows have no bars, but are narrow. Light can enter easily but even skinny prisoners cannot leave."

The social worker announced, "You all have apartment 1A. Very sunny, ground floor, no stairs to climb. Four bedrooms, two baths. If you three guys share a bathroom, the young lady can enjoy her privacy. Work it out. It's up to you."

Mallory said to Can Man, "Let's take the stuff in. Cone needs to talk to your friend." He motioned to Mary to sit down in the front seat of the patrol car.

As Mary got in the car, she said to Cone, "Thought regulations said you can't get in a cop car unless you're a suspect or arrested. So what's up?"

Cone hesitated. Mallory was loading Can Man up with bags and walking toward the building. "Well, you're not arrested. Regulations are pretty clear. Can't be in a *moving* patrol car. See the difference?"

"Yeah, exactly. You suspect me of stealing milk cartons?"

"Oh, no. You seem nice. Going to study at college and all. I went to college at night for five years. Worked all day, besides."

Mary grew impatient. "Yeah. So what's the story? Tell me straight. No BS."

Cone placed both his arms in his lap. "New York's a tough place. Kids come here from all over the country. Escaping, searching for I don't know what. They like to experiment. New life, no parents. Some drink themselves under, some follow sex to go, some get hooked on drugs." His speech was slow and formal like a schoolteacher forced to memorize a manual on helping people solve serious problems with pat phrases.

"Look, Cone, I don't drink more than a couple of beers. Sex? I'm very selective. AIDS is not worth a quickie. Drugs? Tried grass one time. Made me cough till I threw up. See, I inhaled. Finishes me as presidential material."

Cone maintained his serious gaze, "Mary, I could like you. You gotta be truthful. Not for me, but for you. I can find you good treatment. Get you better."

"OK, one down, two to go. Can't be sex. No one beats AIDS. That leaves booze and drugs. I don't do booze. I don't do drugs. Believe me." She spoke in a soft, plaintive voice.

The Buddha was seated cross-legged in front of the entrance with his back to the street. His eyes were closed, but their words came to him stronger and stronger. The manager was gesturing at the social worker. He whispered to her, "This neighborhood's not Central Park West. That guy keeps his eyes closed more than five minutes and kids will snatch the robes off his back."

"It's only human to deny a problem," Cone replied. "If you face it, you can beat it. Specially with friends who care. I know you got a problem. I've got the proof in my pocket. I see those marks on your arm."

Mary pushed open the car door. "Keep what you found. Keep it and I'll die. I'll be dead. You're so smug, so stupid, and so wrong." She slammed the door and ran into the building yelling, "Can Man! Can Man!"

Cone remained motionless. He saw the Buddha open his eyes, stand and approach the patrol car. "May I sit down with you for a moment, dear friend?"

Cone nodded silently. The Buddha did not speak. He noticed the large black radio in the front and a panel jammed with colored knobs and switches. In the backseat, he saw Mary's large green handbag. He reached backward and put it on his lap. The top was slightly open, and the Buddha stared into it like it was a magical cave. Cone saw the Buddha's hands resting gently on the top of the bag.

The Buddha said, "In my country, if a man knows the inside of a woman's own carrying sack, it is like knowing her whole life."

Cone was relieved that the Buddha broke the silence. He replied, "Yeah, same here. Specially here. Credit cards, sales slips, driver's license. You get their age, where they live, everything. Bet you can't guess what I found in her purse. A syringe. Know what a syringe is for, don't you? Know what eight hundred thousand idiots in this city use it for?"

"Oh yes, I know for now in this time people in my country have syringes. It gives life or death." The Buddha replied.

"In this city, it's just death, Mister. I see 'em selling their bodies for five dollars under the West Side Highway. Busted a woman who sold her kid's food stamps for crack. Kid was starving. Starving."

"In my country we have clay pots. We fill them with grain or with water. But some men fill them with alcohol so strong that it stops a man's heart before he finishes the drink. We do not blame the pot for what it is filled with. I have given comfort to my young friend when she uses her syringe."

"You wanna kill her? I should bust you too—aiding and abetting. Get lost. Go back to your damn village. Friends like you, she don't need."

"I am happy you care so much for her. She needs a friend to care for her when I am gone. Please carry the syringe and the purse to her after you have closely studied it. The Buddha placed the purse next to Cone and opened the wide top.

Cone stuck his hand in without looking. He pulled out a shabby red plastic wallet. "No credit cards. No driver's license. Ten lousy dollars. Didn't learn much so far." He plunged his hand in again, "Lipstick, mirror. Nothing special."

The Buddha said, "Keep searching to the end. Until all the contents are exhausted."

Cone plunged his hand into the purse again and pulled out a small glass vial. "Oh my God. What a fucking idiot I am."

"Don't blame yourself, my friend. Go to her. When she first showed me I had never seen a vial of insulin either."

Times Square: Crossroads of the World

"Bud, you know what's the most popular tourist attraction? I'll give you some hints. Not the top of the Empire State Building. Not Rockefeller Center or Saint Patrick's Cathedral. Wait, I'll give you some clues. It's always changing, it's never going to be finished, you can't really see it in the daytime and it just sort of comes out at night. Make a guess."

"I do not know. I would guess the Statue of Liberty. She welcomes all with her beacon of light in the darkness. The clues you gave so generously have made me—how do you say it?—clueless.

"Time's up. Hey, that's another hint, but no prize for you. The answer is Times Square. It's the crossroads of the world. Let's check it out. We'll be there when the crowds leave the theaters. Plenty of action. Nothing like it in the old country."

As Mary moved energetically through the crowded sidewalk, the Buddha said, "So many people. In my village, I walk a few minutes into the forest and am alone."

"Yeah, well, I'm never alone here. Lonely sometimes. Guys rush around. Push. Not calm." She stopped and stared at the

Buddha. Her face flushed red. With one hand, she brushed her hair up out of her face. "I like calm. You hear me, Bud?"

The Buddha said to himself, "While a man desires a woman, his mind is bound as closely as a calf to its mother." The Buddha gave a slight cough to clear his throat. "You will meet those who are calm when you are calm. If you rush too quickly, all seem to be swirling even those who stand waiting for you."

The Situation: Checkmate

Cone heard the crackling voice on his walkie-talkie say, "Immediate dispatch to Marriott Hotel. Times Square. White male with gun on balcony threatening to kill woman and self. Cone, you're in charge. Talk him down. But repeat, man is armed. Back-up there in five minutes. Be careful. No need for dead heroes. Check."

"Check. Check. Be there in three minutes. Call the guys with the movie crew. Get those spotlights on the hotel. Sweep them. Don't blind the guy so he panics. What floor? Check."

"Nine. Check."

"Send fire engine and spread out safety nets. Block off all of Times Square. No cars, no people. Need about a dozen squad cars and barriers. Stray bullets kill. The Mayor will have our ass if some tourist is shot. Check."

"Check. Check. Out."

Mary saw Cone running down the sidewalk toward them. She gave Cone a huge holler, "Officer Cone, how's it going?"

"Follow me. Run as fast as you can. Maybe you can help. Who knows? Meet me up there by the hotel. Here, take these." He handed Mary two police passes, each hung on a long beaded metal string. "Put 'em on. Tell any cop you're civilians with my rescue team."

He took off toward the hotel two blocks away on the other side of Broadway. He pushed through startled theatergoers. His gun was in his holster, but the crowds parted like water as he yelled, "Police! Emergency! Police! Emergency!" He stuck his hand out like a school crossing guard as he dashed across Broadway. Cars braked and taxis cursed.

The huge floodlights that had been crisscrossing the sky to herald the world debut of the final *Terminator* at the Roxie were now gently sweeping the facade of the hotel. Officer Cone stood in front, yelling, "Everyone, move off this block now! Right now!"

He heard the sad notes of a saxophone from a street musician. "Hey, you move it."

The musician picked his cap up from the sidewalk and pocketed the stray coins, yelling at Cone, "Shit, man. Can't even make an honest dollar. Right now is my best time—very best time." The musician scurried off, saxophone in hand.

The balconies on the hotel did not jut out from the building, but were recessed, creating a flat facade with rectangular indentations. Cone looked up about 150 feet and saw a man standing with a woman, waving a pistol erratically. He pointed the gun back and forth between the woman's head and his own.

The traffic heading down Seventh Avenue and Broadway was gridlocked. A long white limousine making a half-turn onto Broadway had been stopped in its tracks by a New York Times delivery truck double-parked and unloading the next morning's papers. Cars trying to sneak onto the side streets from parking garages were immobilized. Policemen closed off Broadway and Seventh Avenue at the top of Times Square. Other officers with bullhorns ordered cars to continue to move downtown.

Crowds formed on the other side of the square facing the hotel. A young woman with a University of Penn warm-up jacket nudged her boyfriend, "This is neat. Bet they're making another Woody Allen movie. I'm not budging an inch. We'll be extras in a crowd scene. Think they'll pay us?"

A perspiring cop lugged two NYPD sawhorses into place behind the crowd on the corner of Forty-ninth Street crossing Times Square. "OK, folks. This ain't no movie. Guy up in the hotel with a gun. Go home. Don't stop a bullet. Get behind that sawhorse back there. Out of range. Move it, now." He swished his billy club through the air and tapped it against his hand like a conductor warming up before a symphony.

The boyfriend muttered, "OK, Officer, we're going. Don't get brutal on us. Policemen are nice where I come from. Lancaster, Pennsylvania. They treat folks with courtesy."

The cop shook his head with disgust. "There's a maniac with a gun up there. Please. Pretty please. Move your ass, Mister, or you'll win a free ride to the station house."

He clicked on his radio. "Riley speaking. Forty-ninth and Broadway secure. Crowd out of line of fire. Check."

A police car zoomed up to Riley and parked at a right angle to the street, forming a solid barricade in front of the crowd. Four policemen jumped out. Three crouched behind the car aiming rifles with telescopic sights at the hotel about eighty feet away. "At this range, I could knock a toothpick out of his mouth. Piece of cake," said one of the sharpshooters.

Their commanding officer said, "Keep your safety locks on. That's an order. Got the word a guy's up there with a woman and maybe two little kids."

"What's the story, Sarge? Kidnapping? Hostages? Or just a nutty husband on a family vacation?"

"Don't know. Hey, there's Cone. He's pretty good. Saw him talk down that psycho going to do a swan dive from the top of the Queensboro Bridge. Cone is cool, but this guy is armed."

Cone stopped about twenty feet from the hotel and looked up. On the ninth floor, he saw the man hugging the woman and waving his gun around aimlessly. This balcony was like the bulls-eye, for all the balconies surrounding it were full of cops with guns, nets and rope ladders. Cone stood alone in front of the hotel. The other policemen on the street surrounded him in a respectful semi-circle about fifty feet away.

He held up the electric bullhorn. "Hello up there. I'm Officer Cone. I'm here to help you. What's going on?" The words echoed off the concrete and glass of the hotel. "Can you hear me up there?"

Times Square was so still that Cone could hear the electric hum of the spotlights sweeping the hotel and the static-filled voices from police radios. Cone shouted again, "Can you hear me?" His voice was drowned out by the metallic roar of a police helicopter that was now hanging in the middle of the Square at the same height as the ninth floor. Cone turned and yelled into his radio, "Get that chopper out of here." He pointed one arm at the helicopter and motioned it away. It floated straight upward and then moved behind the building, invisible and silent.

As he faced the hotel, he began again, "Can you hear me?" The man stared down at him and shrugged his shoulders but said nothing. Cone yelled up, "I'm not here to hurt you. Watch." He unbuckled his pistol and ammunition belt, let them fall to the ground and gave them a kick. "You see? Now you have a gun and I don't. I trust you. Do you trust me?" Cone smiled as he felt the weight of the small snub-nose .38-caliber pistol in his ankle holder.

He spoke into his radio. Within seconds, all the spotlights but one were extinguished. The remaining light focused on the ninth floor, bathing it in a soft light. Cone's shadow projected forward like a giant's right up to the door of the hotel. "Now can you see me without those lights blinding you?" The man leaned forward from the balcony and peered down at Cone but just shook his head from side to side.

Cone heard Mary's voice bellowing, "What do you mean we can't? Let us through. See our passes? We're part of the rescue team."

"Listen Lady, this pass is valid except in emergency situations. You can't walk out there."

"Officer, whenever our team is called, it's an emergency. Think people jump off bridges just on Tuesdays at five p.m.?"

"I know lady, but I gotta follow department rules."

Officer Cone barked at the patrolman, "Let 'em through. I need 'em."

"OK. Yes, sir. But first they sign these papers. Department rules. The papers just say if you get hurt or shot or anything happens, you don't sue the Department or the city. Just a formality, Miss." He handed the papers and a pen to Mary and the Buddha. "Thanks. Good luck. Be careful."

"So, here we are," said Mary. "What do you want us to do?"

"Just stand there. Don't move suddenly. Bud, don't put your hands in your robe. The guy could think you're pulling a gun out. If you get scared or I tell you to leave, turn around and walk away slowly. Very slowly. Even nuts don't like to shoot people in the back."

The Buddha let his hands drop to his sides. He made a nod toward the window but there was no gesture from the man.

Cone waved up to the man on the balcony. "What's your name? I told you mine is Cone."

The man nudged the woman with his gun to stand in front of him as a shield.

Cone continued, "Miss, what's your name? Don't be afraid. Just tell me your name."

The woman lifted her head slightly and cried out, "Natasha."

"That's a pretty name." He recognized the heavy Russian accent which spread out the a's in her name. "Can you tell me his name? Never hurts to know someone's name, and it makes it easier to talk, doesn't it?"

"His name is Vladimir, but we call him Sasha."

"Well then, hello Natasha. Hello, Sasha." Cone smiled broadly and nodded at Mary and the Buddha. "This is Mary and Bud. They came to help you too—find out what's going on."

Cone was relieved. "Husbands shoot wives or girlfriends all the time, he thought, but at home or in a bar, not as a public spectacle. Always a first time though."

"Sasha, Natasha, how many kids you have?"

"Two. Very tiny." Natasha smiled.

"Gee, wish I had kids. Not even married. Are the kids with you?"

"Yes. One sleeps. One watch big color television. Cartoons. She love cartoons."

Cone heard his radio blurt out, "Cone, family of four checked in this afternoon. Vladimir Sharansky, from Buffalo. Trying to check him out. No phone. Street address illegible. Get 'em to talk. Check."

"Check."

Cone continued on the bullhorn, "How do you like New York? Did you take the kids to the Statue of Liberty?"

"No. My Sasha is not happy man. My Sasha is too sad for your country. Wish to leave. Go back to home in Leningrad."

"Well, I understand. Leningrad, never been there. My Aunt Rachel made a visit. Loved it. Very beautiful. Say, why don't we all sit down and talk a little. Bet I can get you back to Leningrad. What do you say?"

The woman turned to her husband and started to talk in a loud singsong voice. The man shouted excitedly and waved his gun. In their hotel room, the telephone was ringing insistently and the color TV blared out the high-pitched laugh of Woody Woodpecker.

The man turned toward his room. "Stop crying, my little one. Push the phone off the hook. I know it makes noise. Push it off and watch your television."

The phone emitted a series of low beeps and fell silent.

Cone understood nothing. "Wish I had studied Russian and not Spanish," he muttered.

"Oh, get off it, Cone. More Spanish crazies than Russian nuts," Mary said.

The Buddha whispered to Cone, "His wife says, 'Let us talk to the young policeman.' He says, 'Must get back to Russia. New York police can do nothing.'"

Cone pulled out his portable phone and held it up. "Listen, I can call the Russian consulate and work something out for you. Just give me your name and when you came to the States. I'll call right now."

The woman yelled, "Vladimir and Natasha Sharansky. Come to American two summers before. Come from Leningrad. Sasha engineer in Leningrad. Here no work. Maybe work like super in basement. No good work. No engineer work here."

Cone dialed police headquarters and had them patch his call through to the Russian consulate. He listened as the officer at headquarters explained to the receptionist that this was the NYPD with an emergency involving a Russian immigrant.

A male voice with a slight accent got on the line. "This is Serge Valnikoff. Second Minister of the Embassy. How may I serve you?"

Cone started to speak, "This is Police Officer Cone, sir. I'm at Times Square. A Russian immigrant, Vladimir Sharansky, left Russia two years ago and wants to return."

"Officer, why a policeman tell me this? Let him arrive to our office. We open at nine and close at four. Do you need address?"

"Sir, this can't wait for office hours. He's up in a hotel room with his wife and kids. He's got a gun. He could kill 'em all and then shoot himself. If you would just come over and talk to him. He wants to go back to Leningrad. Say it can be arranged. If you're real busy, maybe just talk to him on the phone. Tell him to come to the office. Low key. Just reassure him. Know what I mean?"

"Officer, Russian citizens who left Russia gave up citizenship. Many were not true Russians, so we happily let out. Why now does Russian Republic welcome back with arms wide open a maniac, man with a gun who kills his family? I will not tell him we welcome return. He left. I am diplomat. I will not lie. Not even to turncoat fake Russian. As you say here, he makes his own bed and now he can lie on top of it. Office opens at nine, sharply. Good night."

Cone waved up to the room. "Just got an answering machine, folks. They told me in Russian and English to call back tomorrow morning at nine sharp. I left a long message saying we have a family that wants to return home. I'll bring you all there tomorrow. Official police escort. You'll impress the diplomats. So just put the gun down, unlock your door and I'll meet you in the restaurant on the main floor. Is that a deal?"

The man spoke rapidly to the woman who kept nodding her head yes. She leaned over the low concrete balcony wall. "My husband, he not unlock door. Say if police break in door, he use gun to shoot. We not go to restaurant. We are family. We stay together in this room. Food and alcohol in tiny refrigerator. Many chips in refrigerator. Our daughters they like eat chips. We not hungry. We also carry up to this room much chocolate bars. We OK."

Cone whispered to Mary and the Buddha, "Can't let them stay up there all night. I have fifty-two minutes to get that gun. Maybe only fifty minutes."

"Why the countdown? We're not launching a rocket," Mary asked.

"Department rules. The sweet talkers. They call me that. Sweet talkers get one hour. If we fail, a SWAT team goes through the hallway door, the two connecting doors, and drops down into their balcony like gangbusters. Crazy. Little kids protected by cops rushing in with guns. Real smart. If I go up to his room, I'll knock on his door."

"He'll never open it. Won't recognize your voice. All Americans yelling up nine floors sound alike. He could plug you dead. Your SWAT team would just pile in and pile on. Forget that."

The Buddha asked, "Were you ever taught to play chess?"

Cone looked perplexed. Again the Buddha asked, "Do you play chess, dear friend?"

"As a kid, my uncle taught me. I played a lot as a kid. So-so player. Why am I answering you, Bud? A guy could kill his family and you want to know if I play chess."

Mary interrupted, "Russians love chess. A national obsession. Like Americans watch football on television."

"So? So what? So Sasha plays chess? Big deal. Bud, you're losing it," said Cone.

The Buddha continued, "Russians like to play chess. New York people like to make deals. So combine both together."

"I get it," Cone replied. "Like, we play a game of chess and the deal is—I got it—The deal is if I win, he gives me his gun."

"Great," Mary said, "and if you lose, he shoots you in Macy's window. Brilliant, Cone."

"No, if he wins, I escort him to the Russian consulate in a police car and promise not to arrest him for pointing that gun around."

"That's a big fat lie. You'll hustle him in handcuffs right down to Bellevue."

"Mary, you're wrong. A deal's a deal. Have you ever heard me lie?"

"Not to me, but I'll bet ten bucks you have a little something in your ankle holster. Unarmed…trust me, Sasha!"

"Hey, Mary, that's a department rule in these emergencies. What if he started to shoot his kids? Listen, forty-nine minutes left. No time to argue." Cone paused. "What if he won't open the door? What if I knock and he starts to shoot? I can't panic him."

The Buddha had been studying the hotel. He noticed two long aluminum tracks running up the side of the building about forty feet apart. At the top, he saw a scaffold hooked to the two metal tracks.

He addressed Cone, "Our friend who holds a gun will not harm us if we are powerless. Get a chess set. Tell him you want to play a game. Say nothing more. Call the scaffold down. We will all ride up. Mary and I will hold onto the ropes with two hands each. You hold the chess set with both hands before your heart. Our friend will think we are crazy or weak. He will not fire."

"Let's try it. What can we lose?" Cone replied.

He spoke into his radio and the scaffold started to glide down floor by floor. "Yes, I said a chess set! Look in the lobby. Buy one, now! Check. No pun intended. Check."

The radio cackled, "Are you nuts? A chess set? Check."

"No! Yes! Need it now! Check!"

Waving at the balcony window, Cone yelled, "Sasha, you like to play chess? How 'bout a game?"

Sasha leaned forward and spoke, "Policeman want play chess. No open door for trick."

Cone smiled and whispered to the Buddha, "That's the first time he spoke to us. Big step. Half the battle is won when they start talking to you. Fantastic. Great move, Bud."

Mary saw a policeman approaching the barricade with the chess set. She ran to meet him and grabbed it from him before he could reach Cone. "Thanks. Don't need no cops with guns showing running toward the window."

Mary opened the box and took out the chessboard. She started to wave it like a flag at Sasha. "Cone, ask him if he wants white or black."

Cone faced the window, "Sasha, you want white or black?"

Sasha spoke with his wife and shook his head several times.

Natasha called down, "Sasha says police want game. Police bring set. Let policeman choose color. Is polite, no?"

Cone gave Buddha a quick glance. "What should I choose?"

"Please choose white. You will lead the game. Your queen will lead her army made of wood."

Cone yelled up, "OK, Sasha, I choose white. I'm coming up with my two friends, Mary and Bud."

Sasha peered down at the trio, "How I know they not more police?"

His wife leaned against him and whispered to him.

"Wife says OK to come. She say must be girlfriend and priest to pray if die. OK, one game. I black."

Cone slipped a safety belt around Mary and hooked her into the far end of the scaffold. Then he hooked the Buddha into the other end. He put the chess set down on the rubberized floor of the scaffold and hooked himself into the center.

"All seatbelts fastened. Up we go."

Mary exclaimed, "This is an open-air elevator, Bud."

She turned around to look down on Times Square. Teenage girls thirty feet tall in t-shirts and underwear stared down from a huge billboard. A golden bottle of beer poured continuously into a giant mug made of tiny lightbulbs. A TV screen forty feet wide displayed a picture of the hotel and the gunman.

"This is unreal," Mary said. "No cars moving. No honking."

The scaffold creaked upward like a long canoe lifted up by the waves. As the ninth floor approached, Cone pushed a button and the two steel cords pulling the trio skyward slowed down. He gave three more pushes and the scaffold came to a dead halt.

Cone stared at the man facing him over the three-foot-high balcony wall. He was heavyset like a bear, his brown hair had flecks of gray, his high Slavic cheekbones sat under pale blue eyes and his mouth was drawn tight. His face reeked of sadness.

Cone forced a smile and said in a hearty voice, "Hello Sasha. This is Mary and Bud. Glad you invited us up. Never traveled on one of these things before. I guess there's always a first time." He held the chess set out like an offering.

Mary gave a cheery greeting, "Hi Sasha. Hi Natasha. What are your kids' names?"

With a slight smile, Natasha said, "Mariana and little baby name Peggy. Good American name. She citizen. Born in America."

Natasha's albino-like face was framed by pale flaxen hair. Her teeth were straight and white except for one lower tooth framed in gold.

Sasha kept his eyes on Cone's hands.

Cone interjected, "Let me just put the set down on this flat balcony wall. It's almost as wide as the chessboard. It should give good support. Wanna get started? Forty minutes till coffee break. Let's set 'em up." He opened the box and began to pull out the white pieces.

After a few seconds, Sasha reached out and began to place the black pieces. "Set is good. Wood is good. Not plastic like spoons you throw down after eat. I sold wood chess set when left home. This set good."

Cone said, "Listen, Sasha, let's make the game interesting. If you win, I buy you champagne and tomorrow give you a fancy police escort like a diplomat to the Russian consulate."

Sasha spoke rapidly to Natasha, who replied, "Sasha good player but if he lose game, what?"

"Don't worry," Cone smiled. "If I win, he gives me his gun, no free champagne, but I'll drive him myself to the consulate. Is that a deal, Sasha?" He held out his hand.

Sasha kept one hand at his side. The other held the gun, pointed at Natasha. Without moving his lips he said, "Da. Good luck to you. White, you move."

Cone whispered to the Buddha, "Bud, I haven't played in five years. Think this guy is a grandmaster?"

Mary muttered, "Don't worry, Cone. Bud could see the down card in three-card monte. Saw a stock symbol before it hit the tape. A chess move or two is nothing for him. Relax."

Cone's two-way radio started to squawk. He held it up to his ear with one hand as he rolled the white pawn in the other. He turned his back to the chessboard and whispered into the radio, "Lieutenant Flynn, sir, I disagree with that plan...Yes, I'm in charge...This is my idea, not the guy in the robe. Sounds like you have a thing about him, sir...Sure, you want to speak to him?...If he buys your plan, I'd go along... No, I'm in charge, but if you both think your plan is better...I know the police department doesn't take votes on what to do. Give me a direct order, I'll...I'll speak to your boss. He can confirm it. Yeah, I'll put him on...Hey, Bud, talk to your friend Lieutenant Flynn. When you want to talk, press that button. It's easy, here."

The Buddha took the radio and held it gingerly near his ear. In a measured cadence, he repeated what he heard from Flynn. "Innocent dead down in the square. Better one easy clean shot. All finished. Yes, innocent dead all our fault. Cone loses his job. I get thrown out of the country. Yes, give me one minute, kind Officer."

He pressed the radio to his chest and turned to Cone and Mary. He whispered, "Your officer believes one sure dead evil person is better than many innocent dead. Who can disagree? But is Sasha evil? One bullet like magic would kill the souls of entire family. Dear friends, should we choose among evils or do what is right? The risks of being right are grave, the risk of doing nothing is nothing."

In unison, Mary and Cone shook their heads up and down. The Buddha held the radio up and began to speak, "Dear Officer, save your bullet for thirty minutes. Chess pieces can move rapidly." He pushed the button on the radio to silence it. "Let us move around the players." He motioned to Mary and Natasha. "We now protect each other in this small human circle."

The Buddha looked directly at Sasha and said to the assembled group, "Please play the game. Relax for an unexpected finish. No one will lose, but pieces will be lost forever."

Cone looked at Sasha with a shrug of his shoulders. Sasha spoke to his wife. She said, "His English not so excellent, but he understand."

Cone moved his king's pawn forward. As soon as his hand left the piece, Sasha had moved. Cone looked at the board, gave the Buddha a forlorn look and made his second move. Again, Sasha responded in a fraction of a second.

Cone now studied the board shaking his head from side to side. He picked up his knight, hesitated a moment and then placed it carefully back in its square. "Just give me a couple of seconds. Don't want some dumbass move. We just started." He picked up his bishop and moved it.

Like a hawk, Sasha moved and swept Cone's piece off the board and smiled broadly.

Cone wiped his forehead as sweat trickled down his face, "This could be a real short game, Bud. I'm already down one piece. Got any good ideas?"

The Buddha had not been watching the game, but rather staring into the hotel room where he saw a little girl lying on top of the huge double bed watching television.

The Buddha asked Sasha, "Have you taught your daughter to play chess?"

"I teach to her moves of pieces. She like to help to me to move pieces. I tell to her my move and her hand make move." Sasha turned and spoke to his daughter in Russian.

From the room, Mariana replied in English, "Oh, Daddy, let me watch one minute more. Show will be over. I'll come and help you move."

"She speaks perfect English," Mary said. "Even has a Jersey accent."

Natasha beamed, "She speak English all day with friends, watch the television in evening like hypnotized. With me and Sasha sometime speak Russian, sometime speak English."

The Buddha said, "Mariana, please help your father not to lose this game."

"OK, Mister. Ten seconds more, I promise." She gave the Buddha a friendly wave.

Cone stared down at the board balanced on the wall. The Buddha had given him no advice so he made another move.

Sasha called to Mariana who came out onto the balcony and climbed up into his lap. He spoke to her and she picked up her father's bishop and moved it.

"Check. We say check," she giggled. Her father hugged her with one hand but continued to point the gun with the other at Natasha.

Cone made a move to protect his king.

Sasha whispered in Mariana's ear and she moved his queen forward. "My father and I make a good team." She smiled at her joke.

Cone studied the board and reluctantly moved his queen. "Guardez. You want to trade queens, Sasha?"

Another whisper from Sasha and Mariana took Cone's queen off the board and held it in her lap.

Cone responded and snatched Sasha's queen off the board. "Even trade. Not so bad."

The Buddha looked at Cone, "When your foe has a larger army, to trade as equals makes you weaker still."

Mariana smiled at the Buddha, "Mister, is your robe made of gold cloth?"

"I think not, my little friend, for in my village we have fields of strong yellow flowers but not gold under our feet."

"May I touch it anyway? Can I smell it for yellow flowers?"

"Oh, yes, but if you wish to smell the flowers better to close your eyes."

Mariana bounded out of her father's lap and moved toward the Buddha. As she reached her hand over the wall to the scaffold, her body brushed against the chessboard, knocking the pieces over. Some landed on the rubberized floor of the scaffold and others disappeared as they fell down to the ground. She began to cry. "Daddy, I'm sorry. I remember how the pieces were. Get another set, I put every piece back in the right place. I know I can. You mad at me, Daddy?"

Sasha looked at his daughter and his wife. Then he turned to face his three visitors. He put his gun down on the balcony wall and extended both arms to his daughter. She jumped into his lap and kissed him. Sasha buried his face in her arms and began to cry. "Take the gun, Mister Policeman. No bullets in gun. Please come into room." Sasha placed the gun on the spot where the chessboard had stood.

Cone vaulted over the low balcony wall. With a quick snap to open the cylinder, he saw the gun was empty. "Sasha, do you have a permit for the gun?"

"I work in bad neighborhood. Carry gun. Never use. Never put bullets inside it. Just to scare."

Cone patted the gun like a kitten. "Carrying a loaded gun is big-time stupid, but to show an unloaded gun—some punk'll fire first and ask questions later. So, your wife knew it was empty. She wasn't scared?"

"Why she scared? She wife."

"OK, it's no crime to have a registered gun and point it at someone who knows it's not loaded. I'm gonna let my buddies in and explain it to them." Cone walked to the door leading to the hallway.

Four cops in body armor ran into the room with pistols drawn and pointed at Sasha. "Hands over your head now," one bellowed.

Cone stepped forward. "Sorry, guys. Sasha didn't do anything. Licensed empty gun he was waving around. Wife knew it wasn't loaded. Maybe she was scared he'd jump when we rushed him. That's the story. Don't look so disappointed, Flannigan. What did you want, a shootout? Dead kids and four cops firing? Odds are you hit another cop."

Flannigan put his gun in his holster. "Cone, you're a piece of work. Big balls. This guy could've plugged you while you were playing chess and now you let him walk. OK, guys, let's get back to the street. Real bad guys on Eighth Avenue. Let's give 'em a visit."

Cone turned to Sasha and said, "You were winning the game. Tomorrow afternoon, I'm off duty. I'll take you to your consulate, but it don't look good. That guy was nasty on the phone. Say, listen, I have a friend. He's a principal in Brooklyn and he needs math teachers. You could teach math. It's mainly numbers and your English is good enough—better than half the kids. You don't need a teacher's license. You can get a temporary one to start with. With the Board of Ed, a temporary could last twenty years. Wanna give it a try?"

Sasha turned to his wife and spoke in a soft voice. She shook her head yes.

Mariana rushed over to Cone and hugged him. "Momma says yes, so it's yes. Is Brooklyn nicer? Are there lots of trees? Our apartment is half underground. From my window, I just see a brick wall. Is it fun in Brooklyn?

Mary interrupted, "Sure, big parks, a long boardwalk to the ocean. Your English is good. Don't move to Brighton Beach—you'll end up speaking pure Russian. Maybe we can all visit the aquarium. It's like a zoo for fish. It's neat."

"So much concrete in Jersey," Natasha said. "It's like a concrete zoo for people. Bars and gates. Gates and bars."

Wall Street

Mary said to the Buddha, "Remember how excited I got when you closed your eyes and knew the red card from the black? Ten dollars I won. Big deal for me. You never tell me how long you're going to stay in the city. So I'm gonna treat you like a short-term packaged tourist. Show you the sights. Is that a deal?"

"Yes, my friend, you are my guide." The Buddha looked at Mary as she stood outside an ancient-looking stone-clad building. He saw a narrow street jammed with long limousines, all double-parked. Over the din of the immobilized cab drivers honking and cursing in a dozen languages he asked, "Is this building a special New York sight?"

"Sure. This is Wall Street. You know why this street is called Wall Street? Figure it out. Easy, yeah. This building is home of the New York Stock Exchange. Wait till you see the floor of the exchange from the visitor's gallery. Nothing like it in the old country. Center of the financial capital of the whole entire world. And a hundred-ring circus full of two- and four-legged animals—foxes, weasels, snakes, bears, bulls and sharks. Don't get technical, I know sharks are fishes."

The visitor's gallery overlooked the floor of the Stock Exchange. Huge glass panels had been erected thirty-five years ago because Yippies had thrown dollar bills like paper airplanes onto the floor of the exchange causing bedlam as clerks and brokers ran after the greenbacks rather than continue their jobs of million-dollar trades. Sound piped into the gallery was a mixture of yells, curses and incomprehensible bits of words. The floor of the Exchange was a big as two football fields and was dotted with booths, each surrounded by crowds waving pieces of paper and holding up their arms making signals.

A man began to speak to a group of visitors gathered together. "Gentlemen, honored guests, Your Excellencies from the Arab Emirates, the New York Stock Exchange welcomes you. Before we go to the private dining room, I wanted you to see the floor of the Exchange. On an average day, over three hundred million shares worth several billion dollars change hands. What appears as a choreography of confusion is an elaborate dance in which everyone knows his or her role. At each individual booth the man—generally they are men, but there are some women—stands the specialist. The center of the hub. His job is to buy and sell from his own account to keep an orderly and smooth flowing market. Surrounding him are the brokers bearing buy and sell orders for their clients scattered all over the world. The primitive-looking shouting and waving is backed up by computers and telecommunications that link the floor of the exchange to offices of banks, governments and insurance companies in London, Paris, Hong Kong, Tokyo—everywhere."

Mary nudged the Buddha. "Hey, you look like a fashion statement. See those guys in plain white robes? You are Mister Dressed for Success. Those guys look like poor country bumpkins."

A man with a dark suit drifted over to Mary. "Shh. These men rule the Arab Emirates. Official guests of the Exchange and the US government. Petro dollars. Big petro dollars."

"Oh, I see what you mean," Mary replied. "They look real chic. Get the pun, hon?" Dark suit frowned and muttered to himself, "Why do we let the great unwashed come in for free tours? Ignorant peasants." Sticking a big smile on his face, he briskly walked back to his guests.

"Know the difference between the guys running around down there and those guys I beat for ten dollars with their red and black three-card monte on a cardboard table? I'll tell you—Better clothes, worse odds, and big strings of zeroes when they shuffle the cards."

"Yes, my dear friend. As I have heard clothes make the man—or the woman."

The white-robed men were waving down to the trading floor. The Buddha heard their excited words over the click-clack of their swinging worry beads.

"You understand those guys? Funny language with *chhuhs* and *khuus* and *hchusz*."

The Buddha nodded, "I have learned many languages in many lands."

Suddenly Mary's eyes lit up. "Say, remember how you could see the face-down card when I won ten bucks or named the card Can Man pulled out of the deck?" Mary stopped and then, with the grin of a Cheshire cat asked in a slow sweet voice. "You see those symbols with numbers running around on that moving sign down there? See, IBM 148, AA 74 3/8?"

"Yes, my dear friend, I see the letters prance foreword but these are words I do not know."

"Don't worry. Can you see the next AA and its number before it starts to dance on the screen? You know, when it's just resting up, backstage?"

"Oh yes. Of course. I can see them before they make their appearance."

"So what does the next little IBM say?"

"IBM 148 7/8."

"What about old AA? I think that stands for Alcoholics Anonymous."

"AA has a new number which follows it as it waits to appear on the moveable sign. 74 3/4."

Mary stared at the sign. She closed her mouth tight and held her breath. She erupted like a cheerleader as the screen showed IBM 148 7/8. The other visitors in the gallery looked at her like she was possessed. She glanced at the men in the dark suits and white robes. "Sorry. Just got a little excited," she said. She held her breath again until the symbol AA followed by 74 3/4 moved across the screen. She gave the Buddha a big hug and raised one arm like a boxer who had just scored a knockout. The dark-suit men stood motionless like a Greek frieze.

She took one step toward the men and planted her feet defiantly. "He did it, big shots! The next tick of the tape before it happens. This man is serious money. Any of you guys want to try? You." She pointed at the largest man in the group whose white hair and red tie was like a lighthouse set amidst small human rocks.

He moved in front of the group as if shielding them from Mary's taunts. "Please restrain yourself, young lady, or you will be asked to leave. Your friend has a good act. I've seen magicians float in the air or stick their hands in fire and evidence no pain. No one can know the next tick before it appears. It's a wonderful trick. Very entertaining."

"It's no trick. He does stuff like that all the time. Easy! Hey if you're a stockbroker, I got ten dollars. Can I open an account? Always looking for new customers, aren't you?"

"I am a Senior Vice President of the Exchange. I do not have customers. Maybe your friend has wires hidden under his robe and the technician who types in the symbols whispers to him. But it's a good trick. I'd give him ten dollars if he explains it to our guests."

"Go on, give him a quick feel under his robe. He's got no hidden mike. Forget your ten dollars. But I'll give one of your distinguished gusts a free demonstration. You, in that white robe, what's your favorite stock?" She pointed to a man with a short, neatly trimmed white beard and steel-rimmed glasses.

"Of course, it's Exxon. The symbol is XOM. The last tick was 59." He spoke with a British accent in a slow manner as if speaking to a small child with limited English.

Mary turned to the Buddha. "OK, tell those hotshots what XOM does next."

The Buddha closed his eyes. The white-robed men were hushed. Symbols continued to dance along the screen. Opening his eyes, the Buddha made a slight bow to the men. "XOM 59 3/8."

The tall dark suit turned to his aide, "Jesus, another ninety seconds and the magic show will end. Trades come up from the floor in under a minute. Not all the hidden wires in the world can relay something that hasn't happened yet."

Every face in the room was fixed on the far left corner where the symbols emerged. The sheik peered through his glasses. His expression did not change as he saw the golden message emerge: "XOM 59 3/8."

He turned to the Buddha. "Please join us for lunch as our guest. Two hundred thousand dollars has just been made." He turned to the senior dark suit. "Please have them set two more places in the dining room. Seat him right next to me, please."

When they were shown to their table, Mary sat down next to the Buddha. "Ever see a table this big? Enough flowers in the middle to start a nursery. Dig those ugly portraits. Beady little eyes. It's dead weasel heaven."

A well-trained tuxedoed waiter asked Mary, "Would madam like a drink with lunch?"

"Sure. Chivas Regal straight up. Make it a double."

"Certainly, madam."

The white-bearded leader turned to the Buddha. "I have traveled to the Far East and seen men dressed like you who sought alms. The two hundred thousand is a gift for you. Many of your people can be fed with that much money. It is my pleasure." He wrote out a check and handed it to the Buddha. "May this two hundred thousand help many of your needy people."

The dark suit with the red tie whispered to his colleague, "Jesus, with a small piece of that pie, my mother could stay in a decent place for years."

"My dear host who has brought us together, let me give you a small check so your mother can remain in comfort. In our religion too, we honor our parents." He started to write out a check for ten thousand dollars. The dark-suited man said, "Your Excellency, I cannot accept a gift from you. It would look bad."

"I insist that you take it. I will be insulted if you do not. But I understand your position. What is your favorite charity?"

Mary leaned over and whispered in the Buddha's ear, "Himself."

The dark suit replied, "The church. The Roman Catholic Church."

Mary interjected, "Yeah, we met a nice priest at Saint Patrick's. He could sure use the money for something."

With a flourish, the sheik wrote a check. "Payable to the Roman Catholic Church Archdiocese of New York, ten thousand dollars." He handed it to the dark suit.

"The check to you, dear brother is made payable to cash as I do not even know your name." He placed it carefully in the middle of the Buddha's white china plate.

"His name is Bud. Folks who don't know him well call him Mister Bud. You can call him Bud. We feel we've known you for a long time. I've known people like you for a long, long time." She smiled demurely. "Bud, you want me to put the check down here with my ten dollar bill so it's safe?"

With a small polite cough, the sheik said to the Buddha, "We all should trust each other like brothers. What will the Japanese yen be to the United States dollar when the stock market closes today? Will the dollar be stronger or weaker?"

The Buddha closed his eyes. Then looking straight at the sheik, he said, "White is the color of purity. Those who wear white in truth will be the stronger."

The sheik pulled out his portable phone and began to speak rapidly.

"Hey," Mary shouted, "look at them. Every sheik in the house is dialing for dollars. Lots of phoning for a paltry two hundred Gs. This is better than Jerry Lewis' four hundredth annual telethon!"

The dining room was filled with loud staccato voices. Mary said, "I'm learning Arabic. Listen to the words I know from this delightful luncheon: 'London, Paris, Geneva, Hong Kong.' Maybe they're planning their next vacation."

The dark suit came over to Mary. He leaned down and whispered, "Lady, these guys are betting the oil patch with guys all over the world. This is the first billion-dollar three-card monte I've ever seen. Get smart. You and Mister Bud should hit the road now 'cause if he's wrong these guys will be very, very angry."

"Thanks for the tip, but Bud knows. He knows if the facedown card is red or black. He knows the next tick of the tape. He helped me. He helped your church for ten grand. Bud likes me. He must like Saint Patrick's." She paused and her face lost its color. "You're right. Bet he understands what these sheiks are shouting. What if he doesn't think they're kosher? We're outta here. Thanks, big guy. Love to that nice priest who teaches the kids there."

She stood up and turned to the Buddha, "We gotta leave. We're late for our next meeting. Come on, Bud. Just say goodbye." She reached down and with all her strength pulled the Buddha up.

The Buddha nodded to the sheiks, "Dear friends, I must leave. The acts of the generous bring their own rewards with wonderful sunlit clarity. Those whose faces pretend to be generous receive back another more somber reflection when they gaze down into the mirror of truth."

The tall dark suit slumped down into his chair. He whispered to his colleague, "I heard Mister Bud say he'd studied many languages. Bet he understood every word our honored guests were saying. Did you hear what he just told them? Bet you ten dollars he fucked them. Know what that means? The girl is right. He can close his eyes and see the next tick. That's what he did—closed his eyes. Saw the yen-dollar exchange and deliberately gave them another answer—more somber—you get it?"

"Old buddy, I'm not betting ten dollars 'cause I sure as hell can't see the future."

As Mary and the Buddha left the building and emerged into the narrow, shadowy street, Mary said, "Bud, I was just wondering. Remember you told me about the guy who sold herbal medicine to some nasty folks in your country? Did I just see the New York sequel—Herbal Medicine man comes to the Big Apple?"

The Buddha looked at Mary as if she were a bright student who had just guessed the answer to a tricky plane geometry problem. "Oh dear friend, your eyes are beginning to see clearly. Men change their costumes more easily than their desires. From greed to goodness is a journey that cries out for a dramatic push."

The Statue: A Homecoming

"My dad won a prize for something called *Winged Flight*. Think someone just copied his idea and made it New York size?" Mary asked the Buddha, as they gazed up at a fantastic, gleaming stainless steel statue by the Chase Building. The piece of art was sixteen feet high and resembled a flock of geese in flight.

The Buddha replied, "Children make a mountain range small in their eyes so they can make the journey with their parents. Perhaps the statue you saw many years ago became small in your eyes so you could imagine real birds."

Mary walked around the statue and gave it a few taps for luck. It was hollow and rang like a bell. A tiny steel plaque set into the concrete said, "Birds in Flight by Dandan Lightseefar."

She gave the Buddha a poke and said, "Is this some secret message? My dad's name is Daniel, but this last name sounds like a Hopi name. There's a reservation a hundred miles from where we lived. Went there by bus for school outings to see the real Americans. All their English names had this stuck-together long word quality. Bet some little Indian must have seen my dad's sculpture at the State Fair and become inspired."

"Is a message secret that gives forth a name? Do men change names here when they move, as women change names when they marry?"

"Movie stars used to change their names so they didn't sound too Italian or Jewish. But now being ethnic is in. You know Whoopie Goldberg? It's her real name, but she's black and not Jewish. Go figure."

Mary approached a guard in a brown uniform with a patch on his shoulder and said, "How can I find who did this? I'm an art dealer from Santa Fe."

"Lady, I just work here. I protect that thing so kids don't climb it and kill themselves or worse, sue the city. I stop the graffiti punks. But I don't know. Call the Park Department."

They found a phone booth and flipped through the municipal blue pages. Mary dialed the number and told them her story about being an art dealer. "I must find this divine Native American artist."

"Ma'am, which park is the work in?" asked the woman on the other end of the line. "Central? Riverside?"

"Well, it's not exactly in a park, but in a concrete plaza surrounded by skyscrapers."

"You're going to have to call the New York City Partnership of Artists and Patrons. They answer the phone, 'PAP,' like it's some outpatient clinic."

Mary thanked the woman, hung up and called the next number separating her from what might just be her father.

"Yes," said the PAP representative, "we know Mr. Lightseefar, but I can't give you his address. What I can do is contact his agent, Pamela Harrington. Her gallery is at Madison and Eightieth."

Mary thanked the representative, told her she'd take care of it herself and hung up. Her next call was to Pamela Harrington. She arranged a meeting at the artist's studio right away.

"The only problem we have now, Bud, is how to convince her we're serious. You can pass in your robes—exotic living eastern art—and my blue jeans and black t-shirt are a standard uniform, but what if she asks me for a business card and where we're staying?"

Mary answered her own question and dragged the Buddha straight into Woolworth's. They had a machine that looked like a giant video game where people could make their own business cards. She typed in all the information and scooped up her cards. "Look at that! Five bucks for twenty business cards! We're legit!"

A concerned look crossed her face. "What if she calls? Well, I'll just tell her we're moving. Don't call us—we'll call you. I'll tell her to reach me during the day at Rockefeller Center. I'll say my associate can always reach me on my beeper. I'll give her Liz's number. Doesn't matter that she's a waitress."

The next day, they walked downtown to the studio at 92 Greene Street for their meeting.

"Bud, walk faster. Watch out for that dog shit. Know why I want to arrive early?"

"No. But you are leading, so I will follow."

"If it's my dad," she said to the Buddha, "we got an hour. If it's some red-blooded Indian, we can split pronto, Tonto. You know who Tonto is?"

"No, but I see you have a thoughtful plan."

They strode up the block, past all the clothing stores with sleek mannequins in skimpy black shifts, then past signs written in bold Chinese characters with small English translations like "Wang Paper Import" or "Machine Sewing Company."

"This can't be where artists live," she said. "The main art on this street is chained garbage cans bulging with huge plastic bags. Looks like the part of Soho that hasn't been discovered yet. Boarded-up metal shutters. Real quaint. What if it is my dad? Bud, should I hug him or punch him for cutting out on me?"

"You feel both love and hate. For many years hate can build like an earthen mound. Fresh water sent down from the mountain can spread the rich earth over the fields so the crops can bloom."

"Why do I still ask you dumb questions when I'm sure what your answer will be? Guess I trust your voice more than mine."

They pushed on the buzzer and a static-filled woman's voice said, "Come on up in five minutes. You're a little early."

Mary turned to the Buddha and gasped, "Hell, I could be fifteen years too late."

Five minutes later, they were on a freight elevator to the loft. The woman at the door looked like she posed for Renoir—slightly overripe with long, flowing red hair. Maybe ten years older than Mary. She introduced herself as Sonja.

"Hey, Dan," she yelled toward the back of the loft. "That art dealer's here."

A muffled voice said, "I'll be there in a second."

Mary turned her back and gazed out a huge window. She heard the voice and thought that it didn't sound like her dad, but that it didn't sound like an Indian either. She heard heavy footsteps and turned around to see a man with a huge black beard.

"Hello, nice to meet you." He extended his hand to her.

Mary thought his voice was much too deep. She stared at his black bushy hair. It had a couple of streaks of gray and was tied back in a little ponytail. His whole appearance was straight out of the sixties. Mary thought that he looked about as tall as her dad, but more solid. Her dad had been thin—almost skinny. In that moment though, she thought about how, fifteen years ago, she had no breasts and her hair was long, brown and to her shoulders. Now she had breasts, not that they were so great, she thought, but she had them, and her hair was now cut short and colored blonde.

"Hello. Nice to meet you. This is my associate, Bud. And here is my business card." She was so nervous, she handed him two cards.

"Well, Miss Lightly, welcome to my studio. I've not been to Santa Fe in ten years. It must have grown."

Mary hesitated and then remembered that Holly G. Lightly was the name she dreamed up for the business card.

"Oh yes, business is excellent. Every year, more tourists and more serious buyers. I only deal with real art. No painted cowboys or golden sunsets."

She noticed him staring hard at her face. She thought, "I hope he doesn't notice."

She saw long metal strips in piles along the wall. Each pile was neatly arranged. Two-foot copper pile. Six-foot stainless steel. "You keep your studio very tidy, Mr. Lightseefar."

"Yes, when I started out, I had very little space, so I would stack my material—really just scraps—on wooden shelves. I really got my start in a shed."

"I've represented a couple of Native American painters. Is your name Hopi or Navajo? I never can be sure."

"I'll level with you—everyone knows anyway. I made up the name. Might have a couple of drops of Indian red blood, but thought an Indian name would be more exotic and make me more special."

"Oh yes, dear friend," the Buddha said, "What is more personal than our name? A new person can command a new name. I am known by many names. What was your name as a young boy?"

"It was Daniel."

Mary knew. She blurted out, "It's Mary, Dad. It's your Mary!" She fell into his arms.

Sonja took a tentative step toward them and then stopped, realizing that a reunion was unfolding.

Mary's father sobbed into her ear, "Mary, Mary, you found me. It's a fucking miracle. Hey, Sonja, meet my little girl, my daughter Mary."

The Buddha walked toward Sonja, who had started to cry, and said, "We are both honored to see a family reborn."

The Buddha didn't cry. He stood very still and smiled.

Brooklyn: Cross to the Promised Land

As the bus inched along over the Brooklyn Bridge, Mary gave the Buddha a nudge and pointed upward. "Isn't it beautiful? Those cables are so thin and delicate but strong. Held up more than a hundred years."

"That is a long time in your country."

The Buddha noticed a small tug pushing a huge barge crammed full of garbage through the choppy brown water. Seagulls made tight circles high above the barge. Other birds created a pattern of tiny white dots on the mountains of black plastic bags that sharp beaks had torn open.

"We have birds in my country that rest on the backs of the oxen and feast on insects. The oxen are in good health and the farmers are pleased."

"Yeah, I'd call that a moveable feast. Say, you want to know about Brooklyn? It's like another country. Used to be an independent city. It's a one-of-a-kind place."

The hum of the bus air conditioner had stopped. Mary wiped her face with the back of her hand. "In the old days, buses had windows that sort of opened in the summer. Now you can't move them. Built shut. So, I get a couple of free steam baths every summer. No additional charge. It's like a package deal. Bud, how come you're not sweating?"

"My country has high temperatures so we imitate the cactus and the camel. We do not waste the water of our bodies by allowing it to seep through our skin. The water we drink is precious."

"We got a lot of water here. It's free, so people buy fancy water from all over. Bet they take water out of a tap in Sweden and call it Arctic Circle Natural."

From the back of the bus, a man with a heavy Southern accent stood up and yelled, "I wanna get out and walk, man. I don't need no Turkish bath."

The driver, a young woman with short cropped black hair, turned around and screamed at him, "No passenger can get out. It's against the rules. I'll call the cops if you touch that door. Sit down. I only open the doors if it's an emergency."

"This is an emergency, Miss. I preach in forty-five minutes. I can make it by walking. Let me out. I am a man of the Lord."

Mary stared at him. "Bud, look at that guy. Big golden cross. Shirt buttoned up to the top with no tie. Hey, he's waving a thick black book. Must be the Bible."

Mary stood up, "Let us out too. My friend is a religious man. See those yellow robes? He's like a monk." The Buddha looked straight ahead. Hid face reddened as Mary pointed at him. "Stand up, Bud."

The Buddha remained seated. He whispered to Mary, "Wearing robes does not make me special. The one who drives this bus is like the captain of a ship."

"Well, this ship is stranded like a whale."

Toward the middle of the bus, two men dressed all in black with large hats and ringlets of hair falling over their ears stood up. "Please bus driver, let us off. We must say prayers at home to welcome in the Sabbath."

Mary looked down at the Buddha. "This is mutiny on the bounty. First the religious folks, then it'll be the kids. This bus is Noah's ark in reverse."

A young woman with green hair all teased out stood up. She spoke clearly, despite a ring hanging from one lip. "I'm not religious, but I work at a great restaurant. If I don't show, no tips, no job. I want out."

A man with a thin black mustache and a red silk shirt got up from his seat. "My wife. She have baby with her." He gestured to a small frail woman slumped in her seat, holding an infant. "My baby start to cry. Our home close. Let my family go out, please, Miss."

As the driver noticed a muscular teenager standing up, she said, "OK, folks. This has now become a real emergency, so it's OK to leave. Just be careful. Does anyone need help to get over to that walkway?" She pointed to a wood-planked walkway separated from the stalled bus by a two-foot-high wire wall.

The preacher said, "I will help all those who need help to cross."

Mary yelled out, "To cross to the promised land."

The preacher continued, "Will the other men of God assist me?" He stared at the two Hassidic Jews standing in the narrow aisle.

The younger Hassid with a wispy black beard spoke, "We will give our hands to any child or man who needs our help, but we are not permitted to touch women we do not know."

His companion whispered into his ear, "My teacher has reminded me that in a situation of danger, in an emergency, the Law permits us." His companion whispered again briefly. "The Law commands us to help everyone in an emergency—men, women, children, strangers—for we were once strangers in a strange land."

The driver said, "OK, just leave one at a time. No pushing. Let those guys go first to help. Have a nice day." She turned to the dashboard and with a dramatic flourish, pressed a small red button. The back door hissed open. The preacher and the Hassids stood straddling the low fence extending their hands to the passengers filing out.

Mary jumped over the low fence like a schoolgirl. She laughed as the preacher held one of the Buddha's hands and the Hassid held the other. "Wish I had a camera. Great photo op. Religious leaders hold hands and help each other. Who would believe it?"

The Buddha asked, "Such kindness is regarded as strange in your country?"

"Look, the Hassids walk by themselves and the preacher with his young black guys form a tight little group. Jews and blacks in Brooklyn. It's like oil and water. Used to be different."

"In my country, there are Jews who are not black but very brown. Did people walk together before?"

"Brooklyn was tied together by its baseball team. Everyone loved them. Called them the Bums. Like, 'Dem Bums.' Brooklyn was the first team in America to have a black player play."

"I saw in your newspaper many blacks in baseball uniforms. Did they just learn to play?"

"No, blacks always knew how to play. They just weren't allowed to play on a team with whites. But in Brooklyn, the fans—black fans, Jews in yarmulkes, guys yelling in Greek and Italian—everyone loved this black player, Jackie Robinson. But the owner moved them like cattle to California. The city tore down their home, their field and built ugly skyscraper housing. Not a trace of Dem Bums. Not an echo of folks cheering together."

"We build our villages near the river. When the river rises in a great flood and destroys the homes, the people return and help each other to rebuild."

"Well, here the Feds say the flood is a disaster area. Send in helicopters. Drop money and leave. In a few minutes, we'll be in Williamsburg. It's like two countries divided by trenches waiting for the next round of war. Blacks on one side, Jews on the other."

As she spoke, the two Hassids turned and faced them. Farther up the sidewalk, the blacks also turned and watched them walk.

Mary looked apprehensive as they approached the two groups, now separated by just fifteen feet. "Listen fellows. Bud and me, we like everyone. We're not taking sides. Bud is just visiting. Thought I'd take him to see some dance at BAM and go to the museum before it closes. They have a big collection of stuff from Asia."

The preacher walked up to them and said, "Welcome my friends. Come to my church, have some coffee. I will tell you of our latest tragedy: A young girl killed." He extended his arm and shook hands with the Buddha and then with Mary. "My name is Abraham. Abraham Washington."

A young man with the preacher interjected, "It was murder. Ran her down and ran away. Killers…" The preacher pointed his hand at the youth who stopped in mid-sentence.

"Call me Mary. His name is Bud."

The older Hassid whispered to his young companion and then spoke, "The grand rabbi invites you to tea after Sabbath services. Please come to his home at eight. It was tragic. A tragic accident." He walked forward, shook the Buddha's hand and gave an awkward nod to Mary.

The preacher approached the Hassids. "We will make sure our guests will be at your home at eight sharp. There is a deep chasm between us, but the walk is less than ten minutes."

The young black men walked in front of the preacher and his guests like soldiers on patrol in no-man's land. As the group proceeded, they passed an eclectic mix of small stores along the block. First was Sam's, a kosher delicatessen with huge vats of green half-dill pickles and salamis hanging down like edible room dividers, and next was the All American Southern Market with hand-written signs advertising collard greens and chitterlings. And finally, they passed Tropical Soul Sounds, a Caribbean music store blaring out two competing tunes, one from each mounted speaker.

On the other side of the street stood a massive Chinese restaurant, its plate glass windows revealing a hundred tables nearly all filled. Mary noticed blacks and Hassids separated on either side of the restaurant as if by some invisible wall. The large bright red letters on the sign read, "Dragon of Good Fortune" and just below that, in small black letters on the door, appeared the words, "Galt Kosher."

"Folks used to say," she said to the Buddha, "that people who pray together, stay together. But here if they don't pray together, they sure eat together. But it's like different worlds."

"People who eat the same food today may find that harmony in stomachs makes stronger ties than clashing notes of prayer."

"Yeah, well, maybe. Don't bet on it, Bud. Forget it. I know you never gamble."

The preacher stretched out his arm like an Old Testament prophet and said, "See our church down there? We're proud of it. We built a nursery school on one side, a meeting hall for our people on the other and a genuine regulation size basketball court running behind them all. We preach. We teach. We play. We serve all."

"Very impressive," Mary said cheerfully. She noticed the two massive wooden doors to the main entrance under a round blue and red stained glass window. The facade of the church was made of large blocks of gray limestone. A wooden sign in the middle of the wall said, "American Zion Church." Mary whispered to the Buddha, "See that sign? Bet it covers an old stone sign for Saint Mary's Episcopalian Church. Bet there aren't ten Episcopalians left in all of Brooklyn."

The preacher pushed open a small wooden door on the side of the church and held it for his guests. "Please follow me to my study."

The hallway was made of white cloth-covered panels each about six feet high and four feet wide. Each panel was attached to the next with tiny brass hinges, creating an irregular pathway within the vast space of the church. Children's drawings from Bible stories hung on the panels.

Mary saw a picture of a boat resting on a mountain. Two giraffes were exiting the boat. "Hey Bud, look at Noah's face. Didn't know he was black. Did you? See that picture of Jesus? My God, he's black as the ace of spades."

"In my country, our temples have statues made of mahogany so the faces are black. Other statues carved from soft limestone create soapy white faces. Statues made of metal change colors as rust eats them away. So the colors of the statues are illusions, just at the statues themselves are illusions. Do you think the face of your God has a single color?"

"Never thought about it. I'm not a big churchgoer."

The preacher led them halfway down the makeshift corridor to a small open portal. A dozen small wooden folding chairs and a large red leather sofa were set along two walls of a study. In front of the third wall sat a wooden desk decorated with curlicues. The green leather top was barely visible through piles of papers. A half-full wooden bookshelf was set against a large stone wall, and a plain white cross hung behind the desk.

"Sit down, Mary. Sit down, Mr. Bud," said the preacher. "Would you like some coffee and homemade chocolate chip cookies?"

"He likes tea. Call him Bud. Coffee for me. Black. I mean, no milk or cream."

"This has been our church for twenty-seven years. It was given to us for one dollar. Five years of selling cookies and raffles and bingo, we fixed it up. Junkies had stolen the copper wires. Not a single window was unbroken. The only creatures of God who used the church were birds and rats. But now she gleams. The stone is like the pink stone of Jerusalem, and the stained glass window was made by our own high school art teachers. Mighty proud to serve the Lord in his magnificent church."

The preacher pointed to the four young black men who had walked in. "Please meet my four advisors from our community. I am a man of God. They are from the people. Say hello to Luke, Ezekial, Matthew and John. They know the feelings and fears of our flock. They are my arms. They help me reach out and embrace all my children."

The men greeted Mary and the Buddha, shaking hands with a formal solemnity.

Luke was the tallest with broad shoulders, a soft smile and an angular face chiseled from stone. He said, "Preacher Abraham loves the whole world, but I tell him there is anger in the streets 'cause the murder of our little sister. Must we turn the other cheek? The Bible says the Lord is a righteous Lord and He slays with His terrible swift sword."

Mary had sat down on the sofa and she crossed and uncrossed her legs nervously. "A little girl was murdered? Did you call the police? Did they catch 'em?" At the other end of the sofa, the Buddha sat with his arms resting palms-up in his lap. He stared at Luke, noticing a large artery on his neck that pulsated as he spoke.

Everyone in the study was now seated except Luke who walked back and forth in front of the sofa like a prosecutor about to address a jury. He laughed deeply and stamped his foot on the rough stone floor. "Did the police catch them? Damnation! The police give them official motorcycle escorts like foreign big shots. They think they own the neighborhood. Hell, they may own the stores and own the police, but they don't own our people. The Lord. He will rise up and slay them."

Luke banged his clenched fists together like a boxer just before the bell rings. "Ten nights ago at quarter to nine, this gray Caddy limo was barreling down Flatbush Avenue. The big cheese in person was in the back with three of his hotshot scholars. I call 'em parasites. What do they do? Nothing. Chant and debate. That's it. Make their wives work in their bloodsucking stores."

Mary interrupted, "Who is this Mister Big Cheese?"

"The grand rabbi. His buddies say he is the Messiah. Sacrilege. He's just some old Polish Jew. Can't even speak English right."

"Well, your Messiah was some young Jew. Don't think he spoke the Queen's English."

Luke glared at Mary and turned to face the Buddha. "So, it's raining hard. A real storm. Damn gutters overflowing. Our little sister is standing on the curb next to her mother. On the curb, waiting for the light to change. This Caddy comes zooming down the street like they just robbed a bank, tries a sharp turn and slams into Ruthie. Does it stop? No, it speeds off. Her mom called 911. Ruthie was dead when the ambulance arrived. They didn't put a blanket over her. Waited for the cops to arrive. Her mother tells 'em about the limo and the cops nod. Hell, they knew it. They give it an official escort with the siren half the time."

"Did the cops arrest 'em?" Mary asked.

"Arrest them, my...Makes me mad. The Jewish limo guy told the cops he thought he grazed a dog. A dog! Murderers. They sped off. Bumped a dog? They killed her and left. Bet they mumbled their same old singsong prayers. Bumped a dog."

The preacher heard a timid knock on the door. "Come in, little sister." A young girl entered with a plate piled high with chocolate chip cookies. Her left hand clenched both white paper napkins and the rim of the plate. "This is Elizabeth. She made the cookies."

"How old are you?" Mary asked.

"I be ten."

"How long have you lived in Brooklyn?"

"I from the islands. Three years. Three winters of snow. Never seen snow but on the television." She stood in front of the preacher. "Please take." Her smile dominated her face as she rocked back and forth on two skinny legs sticking down from her blue denim skirt.

"Thank you, dear Elizabeth," the preacher replied. "But please offer your cookies to our guests first." The little girl blushed, causing her brown face to momentarily lighten.

Mary took three cookies. "One for me, one for Bud, and one for the road." She took a bite and licked some melted chocolate from her hand. "Real tasty. Who taught you to bake?"

"My sister. But she dead now."

Luke strode to the middle of the room. "Her little sister was run down by that damn Jew limo."

Elizabeth began to cry. Mary stepped forward and embraced her with her free arm. "That's OK. It's OK to cry."

Luke thundered out, "It's not OK." He stamped his boot hard on the stone floor. "We cry and they kill. We will have justice. We will have revenge."

The Buddha looked at Luke. "Can you have both justice and revenge? Do the two live in the same family? Take neither, for revenge leads to revenge and justice if ever found all alone may free its face so it looks only backward."

"Sweet words," Luke said. "You are half-right, Mister. We will never get justice not even watered-down white justice. But an eye for an eye, that is the word of the Lord."

He kneeled before Elizabeth. "Your sister is in heaven and the Lord will send her killers to hell." Elizabeth continued to cry. Her chest heaved in and out rapidly and she slumped into Mary's arms.

The preacher stood up. "Luke, sit down. We fear the Lord and obey the law. Elizabeth, thank you for the cookies. You may leave. Let us talk to our two guests."

Ezekial got up and opened the door for the little girl. "Bye, Sweetie. Your cookies are terrific."

"How long have you been in New York?" the preacher asked. His smile was relaxed as he asked this traditional question.

Mary responded, "I've been here for years. Bud just arrived a few weeks go. I'm his guide."

"Sounds like interesting work. Must meet people from all over the country, all over the world. What's the favorite spot for most tourists?"

"Well, I just started being a guide. I made a sort of special, customized tour just for Bud. I used to be a student, an art dealer too. My dad's an artist, so it fits. Ever been to Soho?"

"No," the preacher replied. "Fancy clothes and art that looks like junk found on the street? Not for me. Took a big busload to see the Cloisters. That tapestry with the Unicorn, the tiny chapel—so beautiful, it gives inspiration. Has Mister Bud seen the Cloisters?"

"Not yet, but it's on my list. Took him to Saint Patrick's. That's the best and the biggest."

The Buddha smiled, "My dear friend, is the biggest church the best? This very church was rebuilt and created by love. Its foundation may outlast a soaring cathedral surrounded by giant buildings."

The preacher said, "Our service is about to begin. Ezekial will lead you to the house of the rabbi. Come again and share with us more cookies."

Luke snorted, "His sermon from the pulpit is always love thy neighbor. Who speaks on corners under the streetlights? Prophets without honor, but they speak the truth. The people are slow to anger, but will rise up."

Clutching her cookies, Mary went around the room shaking hands.

The Buddha nodded to each of the men and addressed the preacher, "In my country, the old ponder and the young act. My country is more fortunate than yours. For in my village, there is little to do and much to ponder. The great floods, the sun that blazes down, the movement of the oxen, rice growing in the fields, the road winding by the river. Here, everything is possible all at once. A jumble of actions. It is hard for you to lead when there is no path. Thank you for your kindness. We will come back."

As they emerged from the church, Mary said, "Ever hear of the odd couple, Bud? Hell, we are the exotic trio—black, white and brown. Know what's black and white and red all over?"

Ezekial laughed, "Haven't heard that joke since third grade. Sure you're not a teacher? Don't hear jokes like that in a snazzy bar."

The Buddha looked puzzled, "I know no odd couple and do not follow your joke. Ezekial, my friend, she is becoming a teacher. First she guides, later she teaches."

The broad sidewalk was empty except for a man with a bowtie addressing a crowd of blacks. He kept waving his right arm in the air as if saluting.

Ezekial said, "Follow me." He turned onto a side street. "Those sidewalk preachers carry hearts full of hate. Works up folks. Gonna get 'em in trouble. Our Luke talks bad too, but he follows the preacher and loves the Lord.

At the next corner, Ezekial stopped. "This is the border. See the different countries?" Behind them, Mary saw blocks of six-story tenements. Their fronts were adorned with rusted fire escapes. Bars guarded the ground floor windows. In the many open windows, Mary noticed people chatting with kids playing outside. Overflowing garbage cans were chained to metal stairways leading to basement apartments.

Mary looked in the other direction and saw blocks of brownstones with white curtains covering the entire span of the window. A freshly painted frame surrounded each curtain. Geraniums in long green trays bloomed on the windowsills. There were no children on the sidewalk, and garbage cans were nestled in low wooden boxes. Bars guarded the ground floor windows.

Ezekial said, "Just walk straight ahead four blocks. The house you want is on the right. Number 45. Come visit again." He shook hands with Mary and gave the Buddha a gentle pat on the back.

Mary replied, "OK, thanks. Next time, bring your passport."

Bowing to Ezekial, the Buddha said, "I am a stranger in your strange land, but I am exploring. You are a stranger in your own country, ensnared by invisible strings. Ties can keep people apart or expand to embrace everyone."

"Bud, you don't get it," Mary exclaimed. "In your village, everyone seems to hang out together, bring each other food, help rebuild houses after a flood. New York is ten thousand villages. A certain street can divide folks more than a roaring river in your country. And it's big-time danger if you're caught on the wrong side of the riverbank after dark. Right, Ezekial?"

"I teach my kids when they're small. When the sun be gone, you be gone home. Explorers get themselves killed by Indians. We all Indians here from different tribes. Never heard of folks sitting down and smoking that old peace pipe. Let me know when you come again. Bake fresh cookies for you." He handed Mary a business card and walked down the street.

Mary stopped in front of the house. "Looks like all the other houses on the street. Think the big cheese, I mean, the rabbi lives here?"

The Buddha smiled, "In my village, the richest man's house had a thick mud brick wall like all the other houses, but he had dug tunnels deep in the ground to store his jewels, piles of diamonds and rubies."

"Dig down in Brooklyn and you hit a subway tunnel." She gave a sharp rap on the heavy metal knocker. The cover of the peephole swung up. The door opened a crack. Mary saw a hand unhook a stout brass chain. In the open doorway, stood the two Hassids from the bus.

"Welcome, welcome. Please come in. I am called Jacob the Elder and he is called Jacob the Younger. Did you have a nice visit with the minister? Did you find your way here easily?"

Jacob reattached the chain and clicked shut the two door locks. The young Hassid interrupted, "The rabbi will be down shortly. He can spend ten minutes with you. They come from all over the world to see him. So busy. So very busy. Please come and wait in his study."

"Why is he so popular?" asked Mary.

The Buddha noticed that the small study filled with bookcases from floor to ceiling had additional piles of books neatly arranged on the floor. He studied the titles of the books stacked next to his chair. "Your rabbi devours wisdom from many languages."

"Yes, he is a scholar, but still very wise," said Jacob the Younger. "He speaks seven languages and reads nine. Two of the languages he knows are dead. Very dead. Why is he so popular? The faithful and the skeptics too—they all come."

"Why?"

The older Hassid spoke up, "Why do they come? Favors, cures, miracles. They come to make personal prayers to the Holy One. Some just touch his prayer shawl, some think he is the Messiah. He turns no one away."

"So he does miracles!" exclaimed Mary.

"He has never told anyone that he performs miracles, yet dozens of letters a week come to us with thanks for miracles. His voice is heard around the world, for he speaks on the radio twice a month. And now, email, from all over. Imagine being born in Poland with no phone and no plumbing and now email."

"Now, that's a real miracle," Mary announced, laughing at her own joke.

Through the open study door she saw people sitting on benches in a room the size of a banquet hall. "That room looks larger than the house," Mary commented.

"Yes, and behind it is a library twice as large with four thousand volumes, and on each side are dormitory rooms. We have over thirty students who come to live and study with the rabbi."

The Buddha whispered to Mary, "His tunnels are above the ground. His jewels are the books and the students who give them life."

A young boy entered the study, carrying a large silver tray. On it was a large gleaming teapot and glasses, each in a lacy metal holder. He put the tray down in front of the Buddha, smiled and left without a word. The young Hassid said, "Would you each like tea? We drink it Russian-style with lemon and sugar. This tea comes all the way from China."

"Thanks. Sugar for me and lemon for Bud."

She leaned over and whispered to the Buddha, "Sweet kid, but he didn't even say hello or goodbye. Think he's a Brooklyn monk with a vow of silence?"

"I do not know. His smile was that of a curious child. In my country, the children chatter. None are silent. In your country, your imagination jumps from a moment of quiet driven by politeness to lengthy vows of silence."

The older Hassid rose from his seat with a polite cough. The younger Hassid jumped up and stepped toward the door. Two men dressed in traditional black garb entered the studio. They stood rigidly on either side of the chair behind the massive desk. Mary noticed bulges under their black jackets and tiny portable phones hooked onto their belts. As Mary and the Buddha stood up, she whispered, "Look at the muscles on those two guys. Must be pumping iron. Bet they didn't get those suntans from studying in the library. Know what those guys are, Bud?"

Jacob the elder said, "This is Uri and Ari. They accompany the rabbi everywhere." The two men continued to stare straight ahead, oblivious to the introduction.

Through the open door, the rabbi entered the room. His bearing was erect, but each step was slow and laborious. There were no wrinkles on his face, though the hand he extended to the Buddha had gnarled veins and slender fingers. His blue eyes fixed on the Buddha. "May the Lord welcome you."

The Buddha smiled and bowed, "Peace to a man of peace." The rabbi turned to Mary. "Welcome to our home. Please let us all sit down."

The suntanned Hassids helped the rabbi settle into his seat. Uri and Ari resumed their positions standing motionless on either side of the chair.

As Mary sat down, she whispered to the Buddha, "Those two are not great conversationalists."

Jacob the Elder asked, "How was your visit to the church?"

Uri opened his mouth but snapped it shut without a word as the rabbi gave him a gentle pat on the hand.

Mary replied, "Nice folks. Real hospitable. They kept talking about a little girl who was hit by a car. They said it was your car."

The rabbi bowed his head and clasped his hands together in his lap. Uri rocked from side to side, the metallic heels of his boots making small pinging sounds.

"It was an accident. A terrible accident," said Jacob the Elder.

"Yes, we were in the back seat with the rabbi," said Jacob the Younger. "It was a tragedy. Uri was driving with Ari in the front. Wasn't it tragic, Uri?" He stared at Uri whose expression remained fixed in a watchful gaze. "Uri, I'm speaking to you. Tell them what happened. We all feel so sorry."

The rabbi said, "Jacob, is it important for Uri to tell our guests about the past, or should we discuss with our guests the tragic present? Hints of violence all around us. We live boarded up like a military base in a hostile land. Let us think. No, let us pray for guidance, for a future. A future built on blocks of love and trust. The Holy One, blessed be his name, commands us to love all whom he has created. Remember in the Passover how the Egyptian soldiers trying to kill us as we fled drowned in the Red Seas and heavenly angels broke into songs of jubilation. The Lord silenced them and said, 'My creatures are perishing and you sing praises.'"

Uri stepped forward into the center of the room. "Most esteemed Rabbi, I try to look forward, but I am bound by the past. Jacob is right. We all feel sorry. I...I am the most sorry. I failed as a driver. The car skidded beyond my control. I failed as a man. I panicked. Was it a dog? Was it a person? If it was a dog, who cares? If it was a person...a black person and I stopped, would a mob of strangers descend on us? Could I endanger our rabbi? No. So I fled. Until this moment, I have lied to the police. To you, Rabbi. To myself."

"Why must neighbors be strangers?" the rabbi asked. "Does not Leviticus say, 'When strangers reside with you in your land, you shall not wrong them? The stranger who resides with you shall be to you as one of your own. You shall love them as yourself, for you were strangers in the land of Egypt: I, the Eternal, am your God.' Thus it is written. What should we do with Uri's truth?"

The silence of the group was broken by an electronic whine. Ari placed his phone to his ear and began to speak.

Mary shrugged her shoulders as she heard the incomprehensible words pouring out from Ari. "Sounds just like those Arabs on Wall Street."

The Buddha replied, "Yes, Hebrew and Arabic are close like brother and sister. Are not family fights most difficult to end?"

Ari snapped the phone shut and waved it gingerly like it might explode. "A mob of blacks shouting 'Kill the Jews' knifed Yitzak the Meek as he was walking home. He whispered something to a policeman and was dead before the ambulance arrived. These killers are not from Egypt. Can we wait like lambs for them all to rush into the East River and drown? I say we must arm ourselves and patrol our streets. No more dead Jews. Never again."

Uri hid his face in his hands and replied to Ari in Hebrew.

"Please, speak English so our guests may understand," said Jacob the Elder.

"Oh, Bud understands," said Mary. "It's just me. So please, for me, speak English."

Uri looked up as tears rolled down his face. "First, the little girl. Now, Yitzak. How many more will die for what I did? Ari, you remember our car ride near Hebron?"

"The worst day. Driving to pray. Arab murderers threw rocks and smashed all the windows. A single pistol shot. My little brother was dead. You fled here to protect our grand rabbi from violence. I came here to train our people to fight. You have failed. I will succeed."

Mary stood up, "I know you don't exactly listen to women, but why not talk before you fight?"

Ari cut her off, "Talk with a mob? Talk with murderers? Never. They understand nothing but force. We will give them something to talk about."

The rabbi looked at the Buddha, "You are a stranger. You are our guest. What do you think?"

The Buddha gazed around the room. Uri was emitting low sobs. Ari was holding the phone like a gun. The two Jacobs sat motionless with blank stares on their soft faces.

"Dear Rabbi," the Buddha replied, "to make peace, we talk not with our friends, but our enemies. Does your Holy Bible not say that the peacemaker stands at God's shoulder while the warrior waits impatiently at the bottom of the holy mountain?"

"A learned reply," said the rabbi.

In an excited voice, Mary said, "I got it! You all need a neutral place to meet. No home court advantage. Ever been to Soho, Rabbi?"

With a soft smile, he shook his head.

"Well, that's great. The minister's never been there either. Tomorrow morning, nine o'clock at my dad's loft. It's at 92 Greene Street, just off Broome. I know you don't ride on the Sabbath, but to save lives, it's OK, isn't it?"

"Another learned reply. Yes, I will go to your father's home."

"OK, Bud. Let's call the preacher." She held out her hand for Ari's phone. He shook his head no. After a sharp glance from the rabbi, Ari handed the phone to Mary. She pulled out Ezekial's business card.

She switched the phone to speaker so everyone could hear the conversation. "Hello Ezekial. How are you?"

"Fine. How's the peacemaker?" Ezekial replied.

"Everything is going well. The rabbi and four of his guys want to meet with the preacher and four of your guys to try... Yes. Great. Tomorrow morning. Nine o'clock. It's 92 Greene Street, just off Broome. Don't eat breakfast. We can all break bread together. OK, see you."

She turned to the rabbi, "OK, it's all set. Don't worry, I'll buy paper plates, paper cups, plastic forks. Everything I buy will be stamped kosher. I had an Orthodox girl in one of my classes. I know the rules. Bud, let's go. We gotta clean up the loft."

Uri said, "We will drive you home. The streets are dangerous. The subway is deadly."

"Thank you, dear friend," said the Buddha. "We will take the bus that brought us here." He bowed goodbye to each of the Hassids.

Sit Boy-Girl

As they entered the loft, Mary exclaimed, "Looks OK for a working artist's loft. Metal scraps in cardboard boxes all over the place, pencil sketches taped on every last kitchen cabinet. Why does my dad save all those old Week in Review sections? He never reads them. Throws out the oldest on the bottom of the pile and adds more on top. Never reads a damn page. That table is all wrong. It's too long and narrow. Wish we had a round table. Everyone the same, no one at the head. I don't want it to be like one side facing off against the other. Get my drift, Bud?"

"We cannot make the table change its shape, but we can ask our guests to sit—how do you say it?—boy-girl. You and I can sit at the opposite ends and we will place a small table to hold food behind each of us. We will both serve all our guests. There will be no tails or head."

"We need a nice spread. Tea, coffee, milk, coke, seltzer. No one will go thirsty. Bagels, lox, cream cheese, hard-boiled eggs. Food seems a little one-sided...Wait, I got it! Grits, collard greens—real healthy—kosher frozen pancakes to just pop in the toaster, syrup and jelly. And orange juice—

everyone loves fresh-squeezed orange juice. Back in a minute, Bud. If my dad comes, tell him to spend the night at Sonja's place. Our guests have more important stuff than to watch her strut around in a half-open bathrobe. In my next life, I could be a party planner—weddings, Bar Mitzvahs. You name it, I do it. Great motto."

"Yes, I shall await the return of the stage director."

"Now, here's the deal. I set the stage, you direct the guests. Be tough. Do you know there are more than a million blacks and a million Jews in New York? We don't need another Bosnia here in Brooklyn."

"Dear friend, I cannot direct. I may see a way, a path or they may choose another trail. They must follow it together or both will remain lost."

"OK, OK. You gotta get 'em talking though. Make them relax if you can, Bud. Forget that director stuff. Be a matchmaker. You have matchmakers in your country?"

"Oh, yes. In our villages, the matchmaker is most esteemed. A matchmaker turns two lonely souls into a single couple."

"Sounds better than personal ads in *The Voice*. See you in a while."

The Buddha heard the elevator gnash its metal gears as it went down. He closed his eyes and folded his legs underneath him. He heard the soothing hum of the fridge and the occasional wail of a police siren.

Leaving Together

The next morning, the Buddha heard distant church bells, and then an insistent buzzing sound.

Mary shouted into the intercom, "Come on up, folks. Ninth floor."

The double doors of the old freight elevator shuddered open to reveal the ten guests. Five Hassids were crowded on the left side of the elevator and five blacks huddled against the right side.

"Come on in. You all arrived together?" Mary asked. She turned to the Buddha who was smiling and said, "That's a good omen, isn't it, Bud?"

The Buddha nodded at the guests. "But leaving together would be the best omen."

"Don't mind all that stuff hanging from the walls. Those metal things are my dad's sculptures. He has a studio in the back, not full of books like you have. Full of saws that cut metal and welding torches to put 'em back together. Coffee, tea, coke, orange juice? What would you like?"

The guests stood awkwardly in two groups.

"You have made the table setting so attractive," said the rabbi.

"Yes," added the preacher, "you were thoughtful to have paper plates." He nodded at the Hassids. "And the daffodils are beautiful. Spring is here."

"Now Bud and I will serve the food." She moved toward the kitchen and continued to the Buddha, "I'll bring the eggs and grits. Bud, you sit there and start to serve the coffee. Sunny-side up and hardboiled. Tell our guests where to sit."

The Buddha moved to the end of the table farthest from the kitchen. "Dear Rabbi, and dear Preacher, please sit on either side of me. Luke, please sit next to the rabbi and Uri sit next to the preacher. Everyone else sit where you please, but with two new neighbors on either side."

"He means boy-girl," yelled Mary from the back.

She emerged with two large platters of bagels, lox, onion and cream cheese and placed each platter at the end of the table.

"Now Bud, you're in charge of the juice and coffee," she said, disappearing into the kitchen again.

She returned with two huge glass bowls of grits. "One last trip. Start eating. Don't wait for me."

None of the guests moved until she returned.

Finally, with everyone at the table, the rabbi said, "I would like to say a prayer before we start and I believe that the minister would like to say one as well."

Everyone at the table stood up.

"Yes. It is our custom as well," said the minister.

The rabbi uttered a slow, melodic prayer.

The minister then began, "After my prayer, we would like to hear yours translated so that we may appreciate it." He then delivered his own prayer, which was short with a strong marked cadence like a hymn.

"OK, let's all sit down. Bud, will you translate the rabbi's prayer?" asked Mary.

The Buddha replied, "The second prayer thanked the Lord of peace for the food. It was a refrain of the first prayer. The rabbi said, 'We pray for peace, Thy most precious gift. We give thanks for this bread from the earth.'"

The Buddha continued, "We cloak our bodies in different costumes but our hearts beat the same. One celebrates the Passover. The other honors the last supper. One event with different robes. Do you not say, dear Rabbi, in your Passover, that sharing of bread forms a bond of fellowship? So let us begin."

"Please pass the bagels," said Ezekial.

"I never had grits. I'll try anything once. Looks like porridge to me," said Uri.

The Buddha turned to the rabbi, "Where were you born, Rabbi?"

"In a small town in Poland. A village. We had our own quarter. A ghetto. When our neighbors drank, we hid."

"And you, dear Minister?"

"On a farm in Alabama. My father worked the fields by day and preached by night. When our neighbors drank as a little kid, I ran. I became fast, real fast."

"My father was a rabbi. His father was a rabbi."

"My grandfather also was a preacher. He traveled from place to place. He finally settled down when he couldn't take the roads anymore."

The Buddha reflected, "Each has taken a long road to arrive at this island. You both fled neighbors and have become neighbors."

Luke spoke up, "We share a street. We are not neighbors. Neighbors do not run someone down, speed away and tell the cops it was a dog." He slammed his fork down on the plate.

The preacher said, "Luke, please…"

Uri interrupted, "Neighbors do not form mobs and kill." He held up his knife, white with cream cheese. "Mobs have attacked me. First they threw stones and we did nothing. Then, as they grew bolder, it was bottles of gasoline. They pushed children forward clutching stones. Men with gasoline hid behind human shields thirty feet from my jeep. We fired rubber bullets. A pistol shot from a balcony hit the soldier next to me. Small children chanted, 'Kill them all.' I fired my gun once and a man fell down. The milk bottle he was holding exploded. Children cried and they all ran. I know how to deal with mobs. They understand nothing but force."

"Shooting children!" Luke yelled.

Jacob the Younger screamed, "Sit down, Ari. Firing guns, Jews killing children. You solve nothing."

"I protect you so you can sit and pray, old man."

Mary heard the harsh ring of hatred drowning out the voices. "Shut up, all of you. Just be quiet. Eat your food."

Ari stood up and looked at the minister. His mouth moved, but no words came out. He licked the corners of his mouth, coughed several times and began to speak, "It was an accident. I fled, I lied. Tomorrow I'll go to the police. If you can't forgive me, it's all right. I understand."

Luke responded, "In private, I spoke of revenge. On the streets, mobs formed. My words fueled the knife. Two innocents are dead."

The minister stood up. Like a huge brown teddy bear, he lumbered toward Luke. He bent over and gave Luke a hug. Wiping a tear from his eye, he continued in silence to Ari. He hesitated, then embraced Ari.

The rabbi arose like in a trance. With trembling steps, he shuffled ahead. He wrapped his thick arms around Ari. He moved toward Luke who took a step forward and engulfed the rabbi in his huge arms.

Mary broke the silence. "To see you guys hug! I never believed in miracles. Still don't. This is something else. What do you say, Bud?"

"Outpourings of the heart drown out words." The Buddha reached out his left hand to hold the rabbi's. He extended his right toward the preacher. A silent spark ran through the room. Everyone around the table extended their hands to their neighbors, forming a human circle.

Luke's face filled with tears that dripped down onto his plate stacked with grits and bagels.

Uri gripped Luke's hand and said, "So we feel good, so we cry. What does it mean? Not a big deal. What's real is out there." He stood up and pointed out the window toward Brooklyn. "Out there we have mobs. Out there I guard the grand rabbi with my life. Should I throw away my gun? Stick a flower up its barrel?"

"Uri," Jacob the Elder asked, "Did you ever think you'd sit next to a black man? Break bread? Eat grits? Hold hands in a silent circle? Listen to prayers together?"

"So what, Jacob. Don't be a fool. When the mob descends as you walk along the street, will you say, 'I ate a bagel with Luke?' Will they vanish smiling in a puff of smoke? Will they ask if you want to toss a Frisbee in the park? I came armed and I leave armed. Nothing personal, Luke. You know what I mean?"

"Sure, nothing personal." As Luke wiped away his tears, his face became hard.

"When I was in high school," Mary interjected, "I read that in the First World War, the troops would have a truce. They'd go into no man's land and play soccer. Sing a few songs together."

"Then return to their trenches and start killing each other," said Uri. "Mary," he continued, "you made my point. This breakfast means nothing. Rabbi, let's go. Thanks for breakfast. See you around."

Luke turned to the preacher, "We should get out of here. Let's wait and see if Ari trots down to the police like a good boy."

Mary said, "I got an idea. Why don't I give you guys a quick tour of Soho? We can leave the rabbi and the preacher here with Bud for an hour or so. What do you say, Luke? Uri?"

The rabbi replied, "An excellent idea. Uri, do not worry. I will be safe here with the minister and Bud. Jacob, you will stare at strange people and strange people will stare at you."

The group left the three men alone at the table.

The rabbi drank his orange juice from a paper cup. He cleared his throat with a cough that came from deep within his chest. "Mister Bud, you see I have young men who want to protect me from others, but they almost imprison me. My heart is moved and my mind is thinking. Guns against neighbors will never bring peace. I can promise both of you that Ari will go to the police."

"That is a good first step," said the minister. "I will send Luke out to speak on the street with a message to love our neighbors. It is another small step, but we need many steps and quickly. Vengeance is not patient or bashful." He paused and turned to the Buddha. "Can you help me? Can you help the rabbi and all of our people?"

"Dear friends, when you go down a long dark path, you need a strong light. If you both walk together, you are a beacon as strong as the sun."

The minister became excited, "I have an idea. Maybe it's crazy."

"Please tell us," said the Buddha, "We all follow ideas called crazy by the visionless."

"Rabbi, you and I, we walk down together seven blocks to the Chinese restaurant. We sit down at a small table in the middle. Mary and Mr. Bud will join us. And behind us, once we are seated, our people will start to come in."

The Buddha added, "And they will sit boy-girl as you have both instructed them."

"Before we start to eat, we will each give a prayer. Perhaps Mister Bud would translate mine."

"But then what?" said the minister. "We need a plan, not just good feelings. What should we say? We need steps to be taken."

"Yes," the Buddha said. "you may light up a great path, but each step must be solid like rock under your feet."

The rabbi smiled. "The luxury of our forefathers to wander forty years in the desert is denied us. Do we have forty hours?"

"Rabbi, are there small steps that our people can take together? We have several young men who are skilled at glass blowing and making mosaic tiles. They could invite the young students to come to our workshop to learn these crafts."

"In ancient times, in Solomon's court, we learned from the Assyrians such skills," the rabbi said. "Perhaps the minister has people who would like to learn to bind books. We restore books with soft leather and inlaid print. Our books travel throughout the world."

"You both share the same book," the Buddha added. "But then your paths separate. When you reach the end of your paths, you will both return to the same place."

The minister became excited. "We have a huge choir. Young, old, boys, girls. We have wonderful music teachers. So must you Rabbi, for I have listened to records of your cantor singing. Our teachers, your teachers. We can all teach each other."

The rabbi replied, "Excellent. What can we do to help the neighborhood itself and not just its people?"

"We can clean up vacant lots filled with tires and tin cans, plant trees in the lots and on the street."

"Trees of life," said the rabbi.

"In my country, I went to a large monastery to seek out a boyhood friend. I came upon an old monk and asked him where my friend was. He said 'Go straight ahead through this field of wildflowers. At the end, turn left and walk through the path in the middle of the forest. Once you are at the end, you will see your friend's stone hut.'

"So I walked carefully through a field full of delicate yellow and white flowers. At the end, I saw no forest, but far in the distance I spied a simple stone hut. I kept my eyes fixed on the hut as I crossed a rocky field. I heard pebbles tumble as a small creature darted in front of me. As I looked down, I saw in the rocky field rows of tiny saplings no more than two hands high. I smiled, for the old monk believed so strongly that he envisioned a forest. I too saw the forest."

The rumble of the elevator doors announced the return of Mary and her group. Ezekial and Jacob the Younger were chatting amicably as they took their seats.

As Uri sat down, he turned to Luke with a slight smile, "We tough guys got to stick together to protect all our buddies."

Luke nodded, "Right on, brother."

"Our walk was a fantastic trip," Mary announced. "It was tense at first, but then some kids with green hair and faces full of earrings started to yell at Jacob. One of them zipped a Frisbee at him and knocked his hat to the ground. Another punk stepped on it and yelled, 'Hit the road, Jewboy, 'fore I step on you.'

"Uri was reaching for his gun when Luke stepped forward between the punk and Jacob. Luke said, 'You hit the road, kid, 'fore the road hits you.' He cocked his right hand like Muhammad Ali. Then Jacob yelled, 'Don't hit him, you could kill him.' That kid took off running. That little Jacob is a clown. He pumped his scrawny fist at the punk's back and whispered in a deep voice, 'Hit the road.' We all started to laugh. Folks on the sidewalk stared at us. Never seen blacks and Hassids laughing together. Just your typical New York guys hanging out. No big deal."

The group seated itself with no prompting. The minister and the rabbi both stood up. They explained their plan. "Tomorrow at noon, right after church services, the rabbi and I will lead the way. We will fill the restaurant. If we are too many, some will stand in the street and eat," said the minister.

"That'd be the shortest Chinese take-out in history," laughed Mary. "Bud and I will see you all tomorrow. I'll be in charge of publicity. Big story."

Set the Stage

After the guests had left, Mary said to the Buddha, "I'll call Officer Cone. Tell him to keep everyone cool tonight. Alert the TV vans and press for tomorrow's shindig at the Dragon of Good Fortune. Bud, why don't you introduce the preacher and the rabbi tomorrow? Say a few words, set the stage."

"My dear friend, you are the stage director. Set a sparse, focused stage. With my yellow robes and brown skin, I will be an exotic distraction for your TV cameras. You have two giants with a single great message—peace among neighbors. Let it be heard with clarity and not mingled with the distant wind chimes of my voice. You are my guide. I will follow you at a respectful distance like a small star in the cloud of the comet's tail. The single eye of the television camera will focus on the comet."

Church bells tolled a quarter to twelve as Mary and the Buddha walked toward the Chinese restaurant. "Wow!" Mary exclaimed. "Look at those three TV vans with satellite senders on top."

Four police cars pulled up in front of the restaurant like a twentieth century caravan.

"Hey, there's Officer Cone. This is big-time. Now, Bud, you stroll on in by yourself. Don't let anyone see we're together unless you want to get sucked into this drama. Hey, wait a sec. Look who popped out of that cop car. It's our buddy, Officer Flynn."

When Flynn saw the Buddha, his face turned harsh. He strode up to the pair and said, "Well, well, it's the druggie and the do-gooder. A fine couple. You like to start trouble? Or does it find you like a fly on...Listen, you bring all these Jews and blacks together with TV cameras, you're asking for it."

"They have asked to sit together and to share food," said the Buddha.

"Like apple pie. You know who said, 'Violence is as American as apple pie'? Black revolutionary." Flynn patted the gun bulging out from his jacket.

"You have an itch or something?" Mary said.

"Call this thing off. It's too risky. Want to have a couple of the so-called leaders meet somewhere, OK, but this is a mob scene. Look!" The Buddha gazed at a group of young blacks ambling toward the restaurant.

"Listen," Flynn continued, "I don't love Jews, but these black kids are animals. Mob of them knifed some Jewish kid to death two blocks from here. The cops arrived and no one saw nothing. Great citizens. Send 'em back to Africa. Send 'em to your home, Mister."

"Lay off, Flynn," Mary said. "Their folks didn't arrive on the Mayflower. Did yours?"

Flynn continued, "Here's the deal, tell the TV the gala feast is off and that a quiet little meeting is set up. Send the mob home. If you don't, there'll be blood running in the streets. It'll make my day to arrest you and this druggie for—let me see—yeah, first for inciting to riot, second for disturbing the peace, and third for conspiracy. Violating someone's civil rights when blacks and Jews fight is a no-brainer. And when you two get out of the slammer, we deport you, Mister. Maybe the judge gives you solitary so you can meditate better."

"You really think they'll riot?" said Mary.

"Yeah, and why find out the hard way? Look, New York's no melting pot. It's a pressure cooker. A racial stew. Maybe you're country's different, Mister. Monks, saints, no sinners, I don't know. Go home. Stop meddling, or I'll nail you." Flynn paused and looked at his watch. "The crowd's getting bigger. They expect a miracle. Save that stuff for Sunday morning. I'll give you two minutes. Make your little speech. Tell 'em all to go home or else."

The Buddha noticed a large group of Hassidic men walking two abreast in a solemn, almost military formation toward the restaurant. "In my country," the Buddha replied, "we have no saints, no sinners, but many monks. Yes, many monks. In my village, most are brown. A few are white—gifts of the English. A few are black—deposited by slave traders. Families cook together. We are poor. We have no pressure cookers, just open metal pots over a wood fire. We share what we have. We do not count or weigh what we bring. All the children are fed first."

"New York is no teeny-weeny village. You don't understand," muttered Flynn.

"Dear friend," said the Buddha with a smile, "New York has as many villages as the desert has sand. But today, let the villages share food. If you put me in your concrete prison, I will thank you that I can meditate in one single spot for many years."

Flynn stood rigid like a statue except for his right hand patting his chest.

The Buddha nodded to Mary and said, "Goodbye, dear friend. I will sit by myself at a small table in the back corner."

"Good. Order some tea or fried rice." Mary reached down the front of her dress and handed the Buddha a few crumpled dollar bills.

She walked over to Cone and gave him a big wink. In a loud voice she said, "What a surprise seeing you here." With a nod of her head she pulled him away from the other cops.

In a low conspiratorial whisper she continued, "I talked to the manager this morning. He cleared out all the tables in the center of the restaurant except for one small table. That's for the rabbi and the minister. Those two will walk in and sit down, then the rest will follow. Everyone will sit down mingled together. You have that portable mike you promised?"

"Here it is." He handed Mary an overstuffed red and blue child's knapsack. "Don't lose it. That's city property and I signed it out."

"Thanks. Hey, look what's coming." She pointed to a line of Hassids walking toward them. "There must be seventy or eighty guys all dressed up in black. And look, marching behind them are women and kids."

A small black car was parked about twenty yards from the entrance. The doors opened and two young Hassids helped the rabbi out. He began to walk with measured steps at the front of the line. From the other direction, the minister led a group of his parishioners.

Men in conservative blue suits walked with women in colorful dresses. "Looks like the Easter Parade. They even brought kids. Hope none of 'em cries."

"I'm sure that they'll get chocolate, vanilla or strawberry ice cream to keep 'em quiet," Cone smiled. "They always have those three flavors at every Chinese place I've ever been to."

As the rabbi and the minister approached the entrance, the TV crews split up and ran toward each of them, mikes extended and cameras whirring.

A young woman with a CNN jacket stuck a mike into the minister's face. "We have reports that you and the grand rabbi plan to meet."

"Very observant, young woman. The rabbi and I will speak when we are inside."

"But you're on camera right now."

"We have waited a long time to speak. We can wait a little longer and speak together," said the minister.

The TV reporter did an abrupt about-face and joined the crowd of reporters encircling the rabbi. She pushed her way in front of him, blocking his path to the entrance and with her mike right under her nose, she said, "Rabbi, the minister just told me exclusively on CNN that you two made a deal. Is that true?"

The rabbi looked confused and whispered into Uri's ear. Uri put two fingers in his mouth and let out a loud whistle. Luke and Ezekial hustled over to the rabbi and locked hands with Uri and Ari around him.

"Please clear the way," Uri shouted.

"Let the rabbi pass," echoed Luke.

Ezekial entered the restaurant and walked toward the small round table in the middle of the floor. Uri and Luke held the front doors open while the Hassids and blacks streamed into the dining room. The crowd remained standing, seemingly lost in the main aisle.

Mary burst into the restaurant. "OK, everyone can sit down. Sit boy-girl. The rabbi said it's OK to sit next to a woman. This is a special day." She paused as the group dissolved toward the tables, seating themselves as instructed.

"That's great. Now that you're all seated, please stand 'cause we're going to hear two prayers before we eat. All the food's been ordered so there's no need to figure a family dinner for eighty from column A and B." She turned to see the Buddha, her translator, standing alone in a back corner.

The rabbi began, "My prayer will be in Hebrew and I will also say it in English."

"Thank you, Rabbi," the minister whispered. "The Lord may understand all tongues, but all those in his flock do not."

The Buddha heard the prayers but then could not see the rabbi or the minister at the table with Mary. He saw the red eyes of the TV cameras forming a semi-circle in front of the center table.

The rabbi turned to the minister and said, "As we discussed, we will welcome your people to learn to bind books in our workshop. I hope they will come as students and stay as friends."

The crowd clapped enthusiastically. Some in the restaurant shouted, "Right on!"

The minister raised his hands to quiet the crowd, "And your people will relearn the art of glass blowing and making mosaic tiles which you knew in ancient times. Yes, come as students and stay as friends. Let us sing together, cantors and choirs. We will lift up our voices together to praise God."

A black woman with the build of an opera singer stood up. Her words boomed out in a rich soprano tone, "Amen. Amen. Praise the Lord. I feel the music flow up inside me. Sign me up as a teacher, sign me up as a student. Praise the Lord."

At one of the tables a young Hassid stood up, "Sign me up as a teacher, sign me up as a student. Our songs will ascend together."

The entire room burst into applause which grew louder and faster. Finally, the rabbi and the minister raised and lowered their hands until the room was quiet.

The rabbi spoke, "When I was a boy, I put money into a little box every week to plant trees in Israel. Our pioneers planted tiny saplings under the watchful eyes of British soldiers. There was no Israel. As an old man I saw forests ringing Jerusalem. I will not see the forests we plant in Brooklyn but our children will plant them together for their children."

The minister added, "The rabbi and I are a little out of shape. Maybe we can't dig the holes, but we will each place a tree in the earth."

The crowd stamped their feet until the cups on the tables rattled.

"When do we start?" a voice yelled out from a distant table.

"Why not now?" cried out a little girl. "But first I need time to change my clothes or Mama will be mad."

Amidst the laughter, Mary stood up. "Great idea, young lady. Let's all enjoy lunch. You all know that vacant lot on Flatbush and Fourth? Full of tires and Castro convertibles? Let's all get there at three o'clock sharp. Get in your old clothes. We're gonna plant trees. Just bring yourselves. The rabbi and minister will bring the trees, shovels and soft drinks. The trees might look scrawny, but we will plant a mighty forest."

The Buddha finished his tea and walked through the swinging doors into the vast kitchen. He gave a word of greeting to the cook, startled to see him in the midst of all the clatter and bustle. He continued through the kitchen and he let himself out the back door leading to an alley. As he took the bus home to the loft, he thought about how Mary need guide him no longer through the city. He would return to the dusty trails of his country and she could lead many over the giant concrete paths that crisscrossed Brooklyn.

Mary smiled at Officer Cone as she left the restaurant. "Know what my fortune cookie told me?" she asked him.

Before she could tell him, the TV reporter pounced on her. "Now we're speaking to the woman who must have organized this incredible event. You were sitting up there with the two religious leaders. How did you get these two hostile groups in a neighborhood full of racial tension to come together?"

Mary waved the tiny slip of paper from her fortune cookie at the TV camera. "Know what this says?" She peered at the tiny letters. "It says: 'Others will follow if you but lead.'" She winked at Cone.

"That's incredible," the reporter replied.

"You mean inedible." Mary faked a blank stare at the camera. "What it really said," she continued, "is 'Follow your heart so old friends become new friend.'"

She turned her back on the reporter and tapped Cone on the arm. "Why don't you come by the loft after dinner? You know the three flavors we feature for dessert. Put you order in now. Say, you know that buddy you have in sanitation? A big truck to haul away the tires would be nice. Show the city has a heart."

"Mary, you're something else," Cone beamed. "I rescue one guy from his perch and you save a whole neighborhood. I should join your rescue team. Need an assistant?"

"No, you know what the Marines say, 'All we need is a few good men.' Me, I just need…"

"Mary," Cone interrupted, "Let's talk later when I'm off duty. Chocolate. That's what I'll take. You got some chocolate sauce to pour over it?"

"Sure, I'll melt all those old Hershey's Kisses. See ya."

As Mary disappeared down the crowded sidewalk, the TV reporter approached Cone. "Officer, what was your first thought when you heard the African Americans were meeting here with the Orthodox Jewish Americans?"

"Well, when New Yorkers sit down and talk together, they can solve most anything."

"You seem to know the young woman who spoke at lunch. What can you tell us about her? What does she do? Where does she come from?"

Cone blushed. "She lives in the city with Bud and her dad." His face became troubled. He began to mumble, "Strange. Where is he? I didn't see him leave. Sorry, Miss, I have to get back to the station."

As the remainder of the crowd filed out of the restaurant, laughing and joking, the CNN reporter spoke into the TV camera, "When the first tree is planted at three, CNN will be there."

Cone slid into the driver's seat of his patrol car. His partner, Mallory said, "What's wrong, Cone? You look worried. Today was great. I never thought I'd see it. What's up?"

"I wonder where Bud was. Maybe something happened. That whole scene and no Bud—It's strange. When Bud was with Mary, he'd be quiet and not say much. But he was in control. Gentle, but in charge." Cone fell silent.

"Don't worry about him. He's no kid. Maybe he wanted Mary to be in charge. You can't tell about people."

Cone turned the key in the ignition and flicked on the police radio as the patrol car inched out into traffic.

Real Party Animal

Mary wondered too. She had noticed that the Buddha left the restaurant without a word and she wondered if his time in New York was coming to an end. Mary had led the Buddha around the city for a month. As a guide she had crisscrossed the city. She thought, "Millions of people like those from Bud's country live in small villages. I have protected Bud from some of the two-legged wild animals that roam the city. Bud taught me to speak more directly."

She remembered how her father had listened when she criticized his latest statue or told him about being poor in the city and not famous. She agreed with the Buddha who said that to chase fame is like eating honey off a knife. The sweetness blinds you until you cut your tongue.

She thought, "Maybe my tongue is too sharp. It cuts easily but doesn't hold honey. Bud's tongue is gentle. Can Man likes him, Liz likes him. Hell, I bet even the sheiks would like him if they thought about it. I like him. He let me teach him. I never taught anyone before. Even my kid sisters—I never taught them, I just told them to do this and do that. Just like Mom told me what to do, how to do it, when to do it.

"Bud's tour of the Big Apple is over. He wants to tell the children in his village how he visited a city where buildings reach to the sky. He likes the dusty road that leads to the cool river where his neighbors greet him like their long lost child. He can sit motionless cross-legged for hours without being disturbed by the symphony of horns, the wail of sirens, the flushing of toilets or rumble of elevators. It's a challenge here, I tell him. Anyone can sit without being bothered in a small village. He doesn't need a challenge. Doesn't have to prove anything. Maybe I should go with him back to his village. Would he take me? I'd go crazy there with nothing to do. I can sit here, look out the window and see the lights of the city dwarfing the stars."

Mary snapped out of her reverie as the door banged open. Her father entered carrying two huge bags of groceries. "Hey Mary, I got fresh pasta, papaya, mangos and bananas. The three of us will eat like kings tonight."

"Dad, I think Bud's leaving soon."

"Don't give me that long face. Let's throw a first-class going away party with live music and strobe lights. Champagne will flow like water. You for it?"

"Bud won't want a big fuss made over him. It's not his style."

"I got a dynamite idea. We'll have a surprise party and invite all his buddies—Your waitress pal, the priest at Saint Patrick's, Detective Flynn, that doctor from the hospital, Can Man, Officer Ice Cream Cone. Hell, even invite those sheiks. Call their embassy. They'll charter the Concord."

"Dad, let's do it. Great! Bud likes people, but he's just so damn calm. Wonderful. It's got to be a total one hundred percent surprise. He doesn't drink, but he doesn't mind it. Sort of live and let live kind of guy."

"Real party animal, your friend. Doesn't drink, doesn't smoke. I'm not holding my breath about sex."

"In his country, guys like him get married and have kids. In the Big Apple, I've never seen him interested in anyone. No one. C'est la vie."

"Yeah Hon, French says it better. I think it's too painful to say in English."

"I'm going to get him a nice present. Something special. No help, no hints. I'll think of something. Party will be next Saturday. Eight p.m. sharp. Bud and I will go to an early movie. He's never seen a movie. I'll tell him to come back here to pick you up for a bite. When he enters—there'll be big shrieks of surprise. I'm going shopping right now. See ya."

Jewelry from Around the World

A huge hand-painted sign filled half the window of the narrow store. Mary remembered that the Buddha had seen a lapis ring that he compared to the blue of the ocean in his country. She picked up a polished lapis stone held by a silver band on a leather thong.

"Beautiful piece, isn't it, Miss? It reflects like a blue mirror. It's on sale, reduced to ninety dollars," said the young man behind the counter. With large hoop earrings in each ear and a necklace made of feathers tie-dyed like a rainbow, he looked to Mary like a hippie traveler caught in a time warp.

Mary shook her head, "It's beautiful, but ninety dollars—that's a lot of bread."

"Every piece in the store is authentic. I bought all of it myself. Every year I spend six months traveling 'round the world and six months right here selling."

"Shit," Mary muttered to herself. "Thirty bucks in my jeans. What the hell can I buy for that? I could stroll over to Eighth Avenue and turn a quick trick, but I never did it yet and I'm too old to start now and Dad would be pissed if he guessed how I got the money for such a fancy gift. Hell, lapis is all over the banks of his rivers. He'd think it was nothing anyway. Maybe something gold. He knows kings got gold. Why not him? Something golden but subtle. Not too showy. Maybe."

She looked at the young man. "What you got in gold for a c-note?"

"Handmade gold stuff for a hundred bucks? It'd be so small you couldn't see it or so thin it'd blow away like a speck of a dry leaf. Wanna see my most beautiful piece? It's real old. Nine hundred bucks. Look at it. An authentic statue of a wise man from over there. His face is rubbed smooth 'cause people would come up and kiss it for good luck. See the detail on the folds of his robe? I bought it myself in a small village way up river."

"Looks exquisite. I could earn eight hundred bucks, but I'd need a couple of days. The party's tonight."

"Hey, I'll let it go for seven hundred, but that's it."

"I can win at three-card monte. Know how they let the suckers pick the black card and win a couple of times? Or they got a shill who always wins and whoops it up? It attracts a crowd. I let 'em win. I bet a dollar—lose. Bet another dollar—lose. Take out a five spot—lose. Pull out a twenty—win, let it ride—win, let it ride—win! Then I stuff it down my dress and run before they come after me to grab it all back. They're mean dudes when they lose."

"Yeah, but how do you win? Two cards to one against you. That's not good odds."

"I learned it from my friend. Don't watch their hands, don't watch their eyes. I wait till the three cards are resting face down. Need a couple of folks around so the dealer won't touch 'em. I close my eyes for about ten seconds and I see the black card clear as day. Win and run, that's my secret formula."

"Listen, teach me how to pick the down card and I'll give you the statue free. I'd clean up big-time."

"It's not easy. My friend sits for two hours with his eyes

closed. Hell, I do the same thing about half an hour a day. It's like practicing."

"Half an hour a day! What do you see, black cards all the time?"

"I don't see anything. Nothing. Just nothing."

"I can't learn just nothing. Best and final offer. Take it for six hundred or leave it."

"Ciao."

As Mary left the shop, she thought of the perfect gift. "He'll tuck it beneath his robe and keep it. He'll think of me. Yeah!"

The Party: Full Circle

"Your loft is big enough for a basketball court," Mary teased her father.

The loft, like Caesar's Gaul, was divided into three parts. At one end there was a kitchen consisting of a microwave, an old whirring fridge and a long butcher-block counter that looked like it had been slashed by a gang of serial killers.

At the other end, three partitions extended halfway to the ceiling, forming three bedrooms—two tiny cubicles and one with a giant king-size mattress pushed under a big plate glass window.

In the middle section was the studio. A series of giant metallic birds made from old car fenders hung from wires on the ceiling. The birds were silver on the outside and inside they were painted in outrageous acrylic reds and purples. On one wall was a nameless composition of plastic that had been melted so it oozed down like a waterfall over a background of rusted girders salvaged from a demolished tenement.

When Mary and the Buddha emerged from the elevator, a huge chorus of "Surprise!" filled the loft. Everyone was clapping and whistling. The Buddha stood in the doorway looking rapidly from side to side at the familiar faces. Mary gave him a sharp tug and pulled him toward the front of the crowd. She beamed at his bewilderment.

She grabbed a spoon and tapped it on an empty champagne glass, emitting sharp pings like a tiny church bell calling the faithful to mass. The roar in the room died down.

"Let's hear a speech, Mary," Can Man's high-pitched voice rang out from the back of the loft. "Everybody," he continued, "sit down if you can find a space not sloshed with champagne, or climb onto a statue—you can't break those metal monsters. Let's hear it for Mary."

He clapped and stamped his feet. The guests joined in. Finally, he put two fingers in his mouth and whistled over the rumble of noise. "OK, folks. Let's all shut up and listen to Mary." He climbed up on a metal statue of a camel in the back of the loft.

Mary was beaming. She began, "Since I met Bud in Grand Central a few weeks ago, my life has been turned upside-down. I met my dad again—hadn't seen him for fifteen years, and I love him more than ever. I made lots of new friends. Great bunch." She nodded to Liz, the doctor and Officer Cone whose face, flushed with drink, blushed invisibly.

"Hey, now even Detective Flynn treats me like a lady! Can Man and Scoop live in a swell place, and I get to see my dad—a real artist—every day. He can bend metal something awful."

She paused and raised her empty glass as she glanced down at the Buddha, sitting on the floor like most of the guests. Through the huge loft windows, she saw the spire of the Empire State Building, lit in rings of orange and blue to celebrate a Knick win over the Chicago Bulls.

She looked around the room and continued, "Now you all know I'm not much of a scholar. Never finished college. So Bud was like a teacher. I can't think of a fancy name for the course. Maybe I got a double major. I was enrolled in Seeing 101, Listening 202 and the hardest course of all: Keeping Your Tongue Still 303. Real hard course. I'm on a roll. My luck has changed since I guided Bud around this town. I showed him so much of the city, he could pass for a native New Yorker if he shed those golden robes. But I think that while I was guiding Bud, he was guiding me."

"You're a great student, Mary." Can Man shouted. He was standing up and waving a giant Coke bottle like a royal chalice. "Remember how quick you learned to sort bottles from worthless junk?" He held the bottle a foot above his head and drank the Coke as it fell with a broad arc into his gaping mouth. A few drops missed the target and dribbled down his freshly pressed white shirt. "Hell, no one's perfect," he muttered. "Now I gotta wash it."

Scoop yelled out, "No big deal, Can man. You can start a brand new policy—wash it twice a year." He laughed at his own joke and then said, "Pass me that pizza with everything while it's still hot. I need strength to listen to all these speeches."

"So, anyway," Mary continued, "I just want to thank you, Bud. I want to give you a little present I got from my dad when I was a little girl. I took it with me when I left home. Hid it under my dress during the day. Never let it out of my sight."

"Hey, Mary, this ain't show and tell. We want less tell and more show!"

"Cool it, Can Man," she shot back. "Sorry, Bud, you know how Americans are. Never let you finish a sentence. Anyway, I want you to take this gift back to your country. Tell the people in your village that my gift flew you home." She walked over to Bud with one hand clutching the gift under the folds of her dress. "OK, Bud. This one's for you!"

"What is this, a commercial break, Mary? Show the crowd the present," yelled Can Man.

She held out her hand revealing the tiny silvery horse. "Remember Bud? Remember in my dream, how he galloped off the ground and saved me from those ugly witches? This horse is my lucky charm. It connected me to my father. It will connect me to you when you're back home. You taught me a lot, Bud. I don't need a thing to bring me good luck. You gave me a way to carry good luck inside me. Thank you."

She bent down and carefully placed the delicate sculpture in his lap. She turned her head away from the Buddha and rubbed at her eyes. Officer Cone placed a comforting arm across Mary's shoulder.

The loft filled with a chant, "Bud saved Mary! Bud saved Mary!"

Can Man stood up and waited until the claps became slow and quiet. "Bud helped me too. He got me out of a goddamn wet tunnel and into a real fine apartment." He raised both arms over his head and beckoned to the guests like a cheerleader, "Bud saved Can Man! Bud saved Can Man!"

Uri stood up next and turned to the Buddha. "Thanks to Mister Bud, I have blisters on my hands from planting trees all over Brooklyn with Luke and my other newfound neighbors. Each year when the trees blossom, we will all think of him."

After the crowd died down, Sasha stood up. With tears welling up in his eyes, he said, "Excuse my not perfect English. Bud make me feel myself good person. So become good person. Happy. New country she become happy country for family."

Officer Cone stood up. At the sight of his uniform, the crowd fell silent. "Bud showed me how to listen rather than jump and judge people. He introduced me to Mary." The crowd erupted into applause and high-pitched leering whistles.

Can Man, like the master of ceremonies at Oscar night stretched out his arm and with a gentle downward sweep of his hand, he silenced the crowd. "Now, Bud, say a few words. What was the greatest thing about the Big Apple? Tell us the three most important things. Hey, then, can you perform a miracle? Fly up to the ceiling through the skylight to the stars."

As the applause started, Mary said, "Can Man, sit down. Bud's not a stand-up miracle man. He doesn't fly through the air. He's not a list-maker." She turned to the Buddha and said, "Your words are few but worthy, so please, we are all listening."

Can Man and the entire crowd were seated and silent. Mary motioned all the guests to sit down.

The Parting

The Buddha stood up to address the crowd. He nodded at several of the guests whom he had come to love as he traveled through the city. Closing his eyes for several seconds, he saw the slow-moving brown river of his village. A river not crossed by giant bridges. It was not crossed except by canoes or rafts with strong wooden paddles. With his eyes shut tight, he recalled his voyages around New York.

He opened his eyes and his gaze moved slowly around the loft, from Mary to Dan to Can Man to Officer Cone to Liz. He was engulfed by the crowd. Giant metal statues were planted like trees throughout the studio. He stared out the floor-to-ceiling windows at the man-made grandeur of the New York City skyline. He was far from his village and the palace of the king, which itself reached just sixty feet, not a hundred stories. He turned and gazed uptown at the blinking white lights strung in a gentle arc on the George Washington Bridge. He noticed the occasional red lights glaring as a warning to overhead planes.

The Buddha walked up to Liz. He bowed his head slightly and placed a hand on her shoulder. "My dear friend, as Mary lay motionless on the ice, you protected her as one protects a newborn baby. With your quick tongue, you allowed me to ride in the ambulance and to stay with her in the hospital. Without you, my trip in your city would have ended before it began. I thank you."

As he approached Officer Cone, he extended his hand. "I know that in your country, people shake hands all the time. In my country, we do not. But dear friend, let me learn your custom as I leave your country."

Officer Cone's large hand encircled the Buddha's thin elongated fingers. "Sorry you're going, sir. I enjoyed talking to you. I learned that what you first see is not what you really get. I sure had the wrong idea about Mary."

"You are a man devoted to protecting the weak from the strong. I remember when you came upon a young woman weak and thin. At the top of her purse, you found a syringe. You believed it symbolized death, but it gave life. Then you dug down to the bottom of the purse and found the gold. Dig deep, my friend. Real treasures are not found on the surface. Dig deep."

"Oh, sure," Officer Cone blushed. "Mary had an old library card hidden down in that old ratty purse."

As the Buddha moved toward Can Man, he saw him fold his arms to cover the Coke that had spotted his white shirt. The Buddha nodded.

Can Man responded with two vigorous shakes of his head, still clutching his arms in front of him.

"In my country, people may work all day to earn food money for their family. In your country, men who move little and make nothing make the most money. But you, my dear friend, are like my countrymen. You move through the streets of the city until late at night. You received not that much, but you shared it with Mary and me. We were your family. There is sadness when families part. But the joy of memory will lighten the night. Thank you, dear friend, for being family to a stranger."

Can Man stepped forward holding the Coke can up as if he were going to propose a toast. "Hell, Bud. Cat's got my tongue. No one ever spoke to me like that since I was a kid. Thanks, Bud. Thanks." He gave the Buddha a big hug with one arm, holding the other behind his back with the Coke, afraid to spill it on the Buddha's robe.

"Dear Officer Flynn," the Buddha said, "you have raised your voice to speak as you saw the light. Sometimes light blinds us. Men adjust and grow. All of us, all of us."

Flynn stuck out his hand, "Thanks Mister Bud. That's all I can say. Thanks."

The Buddha approached Sasha with a soft smile and spoke to him, "When we meet again, we will play a game of chess and we will both win."

Sasha said, "How both can win is a puzzle to me."

"Did not both win in the last game you played?" replied the Buddha.

As the Buddha approached Dan, he cradled the small steel statue Mary had given him and said, "You told Mary and me how you had rushed from your home to Chicago, then to Dallas and then to Boston. When I asked you why you ran from place to place, you said that you had to run after your livelihood. I wondered how you knew that your livelihood was running before you. I wondered if perhaps it was behind you. Stand still and encounter it. Stop running from it. So you have found your daughter and need to run no more from her or toward your livelihood."

Liz interjected, "Old Dan was like one of those pioneers who went to California for gold, except he went exploring in the wrong direction."

Dan laughed and did a sharp about-face like a soldier on parade.

The Buddha continued, "The tragedy of the pioneer is that he sees new possibilities to help people. He therefore cannot take root in the old. But the new is still so far away that he becomes an outcast, roaming the country. He becomes restless, seeking things he may never hold. But you, dear friend, will roam no more."

He continued, "You have changed scraps of metal to beauty. In my country, many temples are encrusted with gold and jewels. I have seen beauty in the simple slope of a clay altar in my village. You taught me that even in your country, with riches beyond the imagination, beauty is born from simple elements."

The Buddha approached Mary with slow measured steps. He cradled the tiny silver horse in both hands. He nodded to her and took two small steps back from the people gathered in front of him. He rocked slowly from side to side and then became perfectly still.

"Mary was my guide in New York. She was my teacher. What did I learn from her? On my next trip from my country, I will teach to my new friends the most important lesson that she shared with me. In my country, we have wise men, priestly groups who devote their lives to studying the eternal mysteries. Mary teaches not these supernatural tales. She taught me that goodness from the heart is more important than trying to discover who created the initial goodness. She taught me that a single person helping a stranger dwarfs the charity of the mighty to the many. I learned from her that I—a perpetual stranger—could find a home with true friends."

The Buddha walked carefully through the seated crowd toward the door. The loft was silent except for the noise of honking horns that wafted up from the street below. The guests remained seated like frozen statues. The elevator stood open on the other side of the narrow hallway. The Buddha entered the elevator and the doors seemed to close automatically like a great curtain. The assembled group sat in silence and then jumped up almost in unison, running to the window to wave goodbye to the Buddha. They heard the elevator rumble back up to the loft. Its doors opened. Empty.

Shouts of "Come back soon!" "Bye bye, Bud!" and "We all love you!" rained down from the open loft windows. Everyone stared down at the street but no one saw the Buddha emerge. Mary whispered, "He just appeared in Grand Central. Full circle, Bud. Full circle."

Made in the USA